# WORKING

# A

# PASSAGE

BY

## Charles Frederick Briggs

*With a New Foreword by*

### BETTE S. WEIDMAN

GARRETT PRESS, INC.

*New York,* 1970

SBN 512-00051-4
LIBRARY OF CONGRESS CATALOG CARD
NUMBER 79-93594

The text of this book is a photographic reprint of the first edition
published in New York by Homans & Ellis in 1846.
Reproduced from a copy in the New York Public Library.

*First Garrett Press Edition Published 1970*

Manufactured in the United States of America

GARRETT PRESS, INC.
*Publishers*

250 West 54th Street, New York, N.Y. 10019

# FOREWORD

On November 26, 1842, the United States brig *Somers* was sailing from the African coast to New York harbor, when its captain, Slidell Mackenzie, seized three men he alleged had been planning mutiny and hanged them from the ship's mast without giving them the right to civil trial. His action shocked his countrymen, to many of whom naval abuses had been only a vaguely understood problem, and confirmed the worst fears of such sailor-writers as Herman Melville and Charles Frederick Briggs. Like Melville's *White-Jacket,* Briggs's *Working a Passage, or Life on a Liner,* was conceived in response to the *Somers* tragedy and grew out of his own experiences as a sailor.

For Charles Briggs, the sea was an intimate part of earliest childhood. He was born on December 30, 1804, in Nantucket, where his father, Jonathan Briggs, was engaged in the prosperous trade with China. The War of 1812, however, made shipping on the high seas risky; the English seized Jonathan Briggs's ship and cargo and forced him into bankruptcy. Charles later confessed to his intimate friend, James Russell Lowell, that his earliest childhood memory was that of being taken to visit his father in debtors' prison.[1]

As a result of their reduced circumstances, the Briggs boys went to sea to earn a living. Charles's sailing career introduced him to European and South American ports, but he found none of them as exciting as New York harbor. In the late 1820's Briggs settled in New York, establishing himself in a business career. He later became a partner in the wholesale grocers' firm of Wood, Briggs, and

Mather, located on Water Street in lower Manhattan.[2]
During these years, he returned frequently to his birth-
place, and on May 16, 1836, he married Deborah Rawson,
daughter of a Nantucket sea-captain. [3]

Briggs published his first novel, *The Adventures of
Harry Franco,* in the summer of 1839. The story of a poor
country boy who comes to New York to win a fortune, it
describes, in comic terms, the struggle of a gullible
innocent to survive among the ruthless confidence men of
the city.[4] Briggs presented a revealing self-portrait in his
first novel; he displayed his anti-romanticism, his wit, his
antislavery bias, his satiric view of the corruption in his
own society, his commitment to realistic technique, his
interest in urban scenes, his sensitivity to the cruelty of
poverty and deprivation, and his narrative ability. But he
so effectively concealed sharp satire beneath conventional
plot line and vivid description that he attracted favorable
attention from critics who were only interested in his
book's witty surface. Acquiring a reputation as a humorist,
Briggs took "Harry Franco" as his pseudonym, and put
aside mercantile activity for a literary career.

He wrote three more novels during the succeeding
decade: *The Haunted Merchant* (1843), an American
version of Dickens' *Oliver Twist,* in which the hero is
morally destroyed by his complicity in the corruption of
the New York business world; *Working a Passage* (first
edition, 1844, second edition, 1846); and *The Trippings of
Tom Pepper* (1847, 1850), a popular New York *Mirror*
serial in which Briggs drew a devastating portrait of his
fellow literati. During this period he also contributed
fictional sketches and art criticism to the *Knickerbocker,*
the *New World,* the New York *Mirror,* and many other
magazines and newspapers. Among his most interesting
newspaper contributions are the letters of a fictional
foreign correspondent, Ferdinand Mendes Pinto, which

appeared in the *Mirror* during 1846 and 1847. In creating Pinto, Briggs combined the most absurd traits of two eminent contemporary literary correspondents, Margaret Fuller and Nathaniel Parker Willis. His target was the hypocrisy and self-deception of his fellow Americans, their pretentious aping of the British aristocracy, and their justification of slavery as an institution compatible with democracy. James Russell Lowell thought the satire in the Pinto letters was too good to be lost, and asked permission to edit a volume of them; unfortunately the project was never undertaken, and the letters are still to be read only in the pages of the *Mirror.*

In 1845, Briggs founded the *Broadway Journal,* a weekly paper of independent social comment and literary criticism, in the editing of which he was later joined by Edgar Allan Poe. The *Journal* foundered at the end of a year, the victim of undersubscription and constant quarrelling between its editors, Despite this disappointment, Briggs continued to feel that a courageous literary review was necessary for the nourishing of a national literature, and in 1853 he persuaded George Palmer Putnam to establish *Putnam's Monthly.* Briggs edited *Putnam's* until 1855, providing publishing opportunities for such authors as Melville, Thoreau and Lowell, as well as many other lesser-known writers of excellence. During the last twenty years of his life, he edited many periodicals, among them the New York *Daily Times,* the *Irving Magazine,* and the Brooklyn *Union.* On the day of his death, June 20, 1877, Briggs's articles and fiction were still appearing in the New York *Independent.*

In his first two novels, Briggs probed the tension between middle-class American imitation of the social standards and manners of the English aristocracy, and the fading promise of democracy. This theme is treated most explicitly in *Working a Passage,* Briggs's third novel, where it was especially topical because of the scandalous *Somers* affair, in which aristocratic privilege had tyrannically displaced civil rights.

The plot of *Working a Passage* is simple; it concerns the efforts of a young man, identified only as B.C.F. (Briggs's own transposed initials), to free himself from the disabling effects of his upbringing by genteel, effete parents. B.C.F., attempting to become a "hard hand" instead of a "soft hand," works his passage home from Europe on an American naval vessel. He soon realizes that freeing himself from his parents' aristocratic social ambitions is easier than winning recognition of his real abilities in the American Navy. This thin narrative thread is all but forgotten at this point as Briggs begins to express his social criticism. He attacks the American Navy for its selection of officers through political patronage and social influence, rather than merit and service. The unchecked authority of military commanders has undermined the civil rights of sailors, asserts Briggs, depriving them of the ordinary recourse of American citizens. The sailors themselves, brutalized by their officers, become further debased as their human dignity is repeatedly violated. Finally Briggs refers explicity to the *Somers* case, claiming that the travesty of justice committed by Captain MacKenzie was the "inevitable effect of a system, miscalled of defense, which has reared in the midst of our boasted democracy, an absurd aristocracy at variance with our beautiful system" (pp. 89*ff*).

Because Briggs was so sensitive to the painful effects of economic inequality, he carried his social comment further than the matter of naval reform. His literary sensibility helped him to see the metaphorical possibilities of his shipboard experience. Like Melville in *White-Jacket* he saw the shipboard world as a microcosm of society, as in the striking passage on page 57. This passage has all the force of its author's incredulity and bitterness, but Briggs could also make his point more obliquely. In the next-to-last chapter, the sailors' spokesmen, Jack Plasket, who resembles Melville's Jack Chase, tosses the sailors' supper overboard; revolted by the poor fare, he prefers hunger to being "fed as a dog."[5] The sailors grumble at the loss of their supper, but they bear privation with some dignity and in the manner of those accustomed to it. The book's last chapter describes a parallel incident, a loss sustained by the privileged class and one borne with far less aplomb. This final chapter was reprinted by George and Evert Duyckinck in their *Cyclopedia of American Literature*, in tribute to Briggs's theme and his skillful timing of a humorous climax. Adding slapstick to the comic effects of caricature, Briggs allows his democrats to go hungry, but permits them a moral victory over the plutocrats of American society.

Although social injustice was Briggs's subject in *Working a Passage*, he also approached the book with a defined literary purpose. "I was seized one day," he confessed to Lowell, "with a philanthropic desire to furnish the great reading world with a little bit of simple, truthful prose as an antidote to the outrageous distortions of truth which the poor world is swallowing day after day in the shape of Eugene Sueisms, Howittisms, and Sedgwickisms, where little country girls behave like incarnate angels and grown-up men like incarnate devils; for to me, impossible goodness is as offensive as impossible wickedness."[6] Briggs's realism is most effective in his description of Liverpool: of the poor who serve their reminiscences for dessert; of the fishwomen "too disheartened to cry their scaly commodities." These passages, added to the fuller treatment of New York in *The Adventures of Harry Franco* and *The Trippings of Tom Pepper*, demonstrate that Briggs, like William Dean Howells, Stephen Crane,

Theodore Dreiser and Thomas Wolfe, felt the impact of city scenes strongly enough to record them with passionate truthfulness. While *Working a Passage* is the minor novel of a minor writer, it is compelling reading for this attempt at realism, for its legitimate social criticism, and finally, for its witty, intelligent attack on the same absurd pretentiousness that later bemused Mark Twain.

[1] See Briggs to Lowell, unpublished letter dated March 19, 1845, deposited in the Page Papers, Archives of American Art, Detroit, Michigan.

[2] This information was gleaned from Brooklyn *City Directories* and Doggett's *New York City Business Directory* for the years 1820-1855.

[3] Vital Records of Nantucket and Pollard Papers, Nantucket Atheneum, Nantucket, Massachusetts.

[4] See my foreword to the facsimile edition of *Harry Franco* in the present series.

[5] This chapter was added to the second edition (1846).

[6] Briggs to Lowell, unpublished letter dated July 9, 1844, deposited in the Page Papers, Archives of American Art, Detroit, Michigan.

## Textual Note

*Working a Passage* was first published by John Allen of New York in 1844. Two years later Homans & Ellis of New York printed a second edition, with the addition of the next-to-last chapter. Because of this significant addition, the second edition has been chosen for reproduction here.

## Bibliography

There are no published full-length biographies or critical studies of Briggs; the following is a selected list of books or articles which treat Briggs's life or work.

Edward Cary. *George William Curtis.* New York, 1894.

John J. Cawelti. *Apostles of the Self-Made Man.* Chicago, 1965.

Martin Duberman. *James Russell Lowell.* New York, 1967.

Heyward Ehrlich. "Charles Frederick Briggs and Lowell's *Fable for Critics,*" *Modern Language Quarterly,* XXVIII (September, 1967), 329-341.

_____."*The Broadway Journal* — Briggs's Dilemma and Poe's Strategy," *Bulletin of the New York Public Library,* LXXIII (February, 1969), 74-93.

Perry Miller. *The Raven and the Whale.* New York, 1956.

Horace Scudder. *James Russell Lowell.* New York, 1901.

Joshua Taylor. *William Page, The American Titian.* Chicago, 1967.

Bette Weidman. *Charles Frederick Briggs, A Critical Biography.* Unpublished dissertation, Columbia University, 1968.

_____. "*The Broadway Journal:* A Casualty of Abolition Politics," *Bulletin of the New York Public Library,* LXXIII (Feburary, 1969), 94-113.

George Woodberry. *The Life of Edgar Allan Poe.* Boston, 1909.

Bette S. Weidman
*Queens University*

NEW-YORK PACKET SHIP, OFF THE QUARANTINE.

# WORKING A PASSAGE;

OR,

## LIFE IN A LINER.

(PUBLISHED FOR THE BENEFIT OF YOUNG TRAVELLERS.)

NEW EDITION.

New-York:

HOMANS & ELLIS, 295 BROADWAY.

1846.

Stereotyped by J. Van Norden & Co.
60 William-street.

# CONTENTS.

# CHAPTER I.

A NEW book is not so great a rarity in these days as to require an apology for its appearance; but when an author has a reasonable excuse to offer for his work, it is better to give it than to put the reader to the trouble of divining excuses for him. Besides, I cannot but think, judging from my own feelings, that the public will be more ready to listen patiently to any one who challenges their attention, when the challenger explains his motives for so doing in the outset.

My motive, then, in writing and publishing this little book, is to furnish a hint to those young men, very numerous I fear they are, who sometimes find themselves suddenly deprived of their accustomed means of support, and before they become used to standing alone, fall so heavily to the ground, as to be unable ever to rise again. I can conceive nothing more melancholy, than to see one human being dependent upon another for support, when nature has not deprived him of the lawful means of supporting himself. In one sense, men are all dependent upon each other; and therefore, whosoever receives anything from his fellow creatures should return an equivalent, or he is not worthy to remain among them; he is a useless member in the arch of society, a block that gives neither ornament nor strength, and should therefore be removed.

No man should ever hesitate, either to ask, or receive aid from others, who is conscious of a desire to aid himself. In working for himself, he has work-

1*

ed for others. The most selfish people do a vast deal
of good to their neighbours without knowing it. The
farmer, who from motives of intense selfishness, tills
his ground so that it produces a double crop, light-
ens the burden of his poorer neighbour, who is in
consequence enabled to buy cheaper bread. Society has nothing to ask of its members, but that each
one should be intensely selfish and provide for his
own necessities.

Though an honest man should never blush to receive aid, yet nothing can be more gratifying to such
an one, than the consciousness of having extricated
himself from pecuniary embarrassments by the sweat
of his own brow ; while the most depressing condition that an intelligent mind can be placed in, is
that of dependence upon friends, or of indebtedness
to any body. To have eaten the bread of honest
industry—the industry that causes the sweat to start
from the brow—is to have tasted one of the greatest
enjoyments of life. How many miss it, who dream
of having skimmed the cream of human felicities !
Many rich men seek after this enjoyment by boisterous amusements, and violent exercises in the
open air ; but they mistake the negative pleasure of
repose after weariness, for the positive zest of enjoyment, which is the sure reward of industry.
" Labour for labour's sake is against nature," says
Locke. They mistake fatigue of the body for the
refreshment of mind which only an honest purpose
can give to labour. A man may strengthen the
muscles of his arms by the use of dumb-bells, but
such exercise will enfeeble his mind as much as
though he wasted his time in toying with a doll.

Many young men, both in town and country, have
disgracefully resorted to fraud and meanness to save
themselves from what they have falsely considered
the degradation of labour ; and for so doing they
have not been so much open to blame as the in-

structors who instilled such pernicious ambition into
their minds. Society should be most lenient to the
vices which its own rules engender; but in an ill-
organized community, everything is distorted from
its right use, and punishments and rewards are
meted out to the greatest extent, where they are
least deserved. Our statute law makes no distinction between the man who eats his bread by the
sweat of his own brow, and him who eats it by the
sweat of another's. Not so our common law—our
law of daily habit—which is read by all men, and
therefore most regarded. The soft hands and the
hard hands are distinct orders in our social constitu-
tion ; where all men are very far from being equal.
It was my lot to be reared among the former, and
to imbibe all their prejudices, and be swayed by all
the effeminate customs of the caste. For this I do
not blame those who had the direction of my education. It would be impossible, by precept, to coun-
teract the effect which the practice of the world has
upon the minds of the young. The only true teach
ing for youth is example.

Happily, I was compelled to learn a lesson in regard to these things, before my mind had become so
hardened in the mould in which it was first formed,
as to be incapable of receiving other impressions.

## CHAPTER II.

### GETTING ADRIFT.

In the beginning of July, 1832, New-York was thrown into a consternation by the appearance of the Asiatic cholera, and all who had the means of leaving the city, began to make arrangements for their departure. Being an only son, I was a pet with my mother, who urged my father to send me away until the threatened pestilence should be passed. For my father's occupations were of a nature that compelled him to remain in the city, and she refused to leave without him. But where should I go? Since the terrible epidemic had made its appearance upon the continent, it was impossible to anticipate the points of its attack; and there seemed as much danger in visiting any neighbouring city, as in remaining at home. A place of safety immediately suggested itself to my own mind,—Europe. At first my father opposed it strongly. I was in my twentieth year, and it had been arranged that I should go into business with a fellow-clerk a few years older than myself, when I reached my majority. He was apprehensive that I should fall into loose habits; the very sound of Europe seemed to alarm him with vague notions of uncertain expenses. He had an idea that one could not go to Europe without associating with the nobility and kings and emperors. But after making some inquiries among the importers of his acquaintance, he became satisfied that one might visit Europe without mixing with such expensive company; and finding that travelling abroad would cost very little more than travelling at home, he consented to my going.

My father's misapprehension about the kind of company that I should fall into in Europe, was not so much out of the way as some may think. He was a very diligent reader of newspapers, but he rarely read anything else; and as the health and doings of princes and the nobility form the greater portion of the European news dealt out to the public by the morning and evening presses, these personages naturally came first into his mind when Europe was mentioned; just as one would think of being introduced to the Grand Seignior, if he should talk of going to Constantinople.

My mother was very anxious that I should visit Europe, not only for my own improvement, but for the credit of the family. None of our name had gone back to the father-land since our ancestors came over two hundred years before. It was the 2d of July when my going was determined upon, and a packet, the Philadelphia, was to sail on the 10th for London; I engaged my passage immediately, and devoted the intervening time to preparations for my journey. At first it was determined that I should go no farther than Paris, and return as soon as I heard of the disappearance of the cholera; but as going to Europe was not likely to be an event of very frequent occurrence in my life, I prevailed upon my father to allow me to remain abroad a year, for I had a very strong desire to visit Florence and Rome. When the day of my departure arrived, I was half inclined to remain, for the pestilence had begun to spread to a very alarming extent, and I took leave of my parents and sisters with a heavy heart.

We had a tedious passage across the Atlantic, at least it seemed tedious to me, for I had never been at sea before, and I suffered a good deal from sea-sickness. The ship was new and her accommodations were excellent, but there was a woful difference between the narrow state-room of a ship's cabin, and the spacious chamber I had always occupied at home. And then the table! capital for a ship, no doubt; but I thought it a great hardship to eat my dinner without fresh vegetables, and to drink stale water; but worse than all, the uncertainty when I took a cup of coffee or a spoonful of soup in my hand, whether it would go down the inside or outside of my throat. These things were the merest trifles, scarcely worth a passing thought with an old traveller, but I thought they were very serious matters, and looked upon myself as quite a hero for enduring them.

There were some forty or fifty men, women and children, cooped up in a little hole between decks, forward of the cabin, called the steerage, who slept in hanging shelves eight or ten in a tier, and cooked their own food, when the weather would admit of a fire being kindled in the galley allotted to their use, who doubtless looked upon the passengers in the cabin as enjoying quite a Heaven afloat. But, never having suffered any discomforts myself, I could not feel for those who did, and therefore it never occurred to me that I was enjoying privileges which were denied to others, who were quite as worthy as myself. I have since looked back with amazement when I have thought of the apathy of feeling with which I regarded delicate looking women enduring hardships that I should have considered unbearable in my own case, and wondered that I could not perceive what a favoured creature I was. But the fish do not know that there is such an element as water, until they are drawn out of it.

The life of a passenger, whether in the cabin or steerage, on board of a packet ship, can hardly be called life; it is a state of half way existence between dreaming and waking, and is not the kind of "life" which I intend to describe in these pages. Eating and sleeping are the only employments which a passenger can attend to, and these are never enjoyed with a zest, because they are indulged in too freely. The only event which really appears like life on the ocean, to a mere spectator, is a death. Death is always so near, so solemn, so positive and thought-compelling, that wherever he may come he forces us to remember that we are living beings, and that we have interests at stake beyond the little affairs which surround us. I was made fully sensible of the truth of these trite reflections before our passage was half made. In the cabin there was a lively young gentleman, who, like myself, had left New-York to avoid the cholera. He had been at sea before, and was almost the only passenger among us who did not suffer from sea-sickness. One day after dinner he stood by the fife-rail of the mainmast, smoking a cigar and chatting with Captain C ——, when an iron marlinespike fell from the hands of a sailor who was at work at the head of the topmast, and struck him on the crown of his head. The sharp end of the marlinespike buried itself two or three inches in his brain. He died, almost instantly, and was buried the same evening. It was a calm, moonlight night, the ship was hardly moving through the water, but the main topsail was thrown aback according to sea etiquette; the peak of the spanker was lowered, the corpse, sewed up in a canvass shroud, with a heavy weight attached to the feet, was placed upon a plank with an end resting upon the taffrail. Our captain read the services for the burial of the dead at sea, while the crew and passengers gathered round with uncovered heads; when the last amen was pronounced, the plank was raised and the body of our companion plunged into the ocean. I could not see it, but looking over the taffrail immediately after,

I saw a few bubbles rise and burst, which seemed to say, this is life.

"Hard up your helm; wear round!" cried the mate, and we were once more on our way.

We arrived at Spithead on the 6th day of August, and I hurried ashore in the first boat that came off from Portsmouth, quite as anxious to get something comfortable to eat and drink, as to step upon English soil. Some of the passengers remained on board the ship until she reached London. But I got there a day or two ahead of her, and when she hauled into the St. Katharine's dock, I went on board of her with some such feelings of curiosity as a released prisoner may be supposed to experience in revisiting the place of his confinement, after tasting the sweets of freedom. Disagreeable as my recollections of the ship were, a few days' acquaintance with Mivart's, for an inconsiderate friend of my father's had recommended me to lodge at that expensive hotel, caused her to appear so very uncomfortable in my eyes, that I only took one look at my old stateroom, with its narrow berth and blue morocco curtains, and shuddering at the thought of being compelled to squeeze myself into such contracted quarters again, I leaped ashore, and blessed myself that I was on dry land.

I had determined to spend the summer and autumn in England and Scotland, and not visit Paris until November, when I expected to receive letters from home, and a bill of credit on Hottinguer & Co., which my father had promised to send me. I had the good fortune to make some pleasant acquaintances in Scotland, who detained me longer than I intended remaining there, so that I did not reach Paris until the middle of November, when my money was nearly spent. I called upon Hottinguer & Co. the day after my arrival, and found letters that had been lying there for more than a month. They contained no bill of credit, but they informed me of my father's death. He was almost the last victim of the cholera. In addition to this distressing news, I was informed by a letter from the young gentleman with whom I was to have formed a business connection, that my father had died insolvent, but that he would, on my return, complete the arrangements for our partnership, without regard to the deficiency of capital on my part, which he knew this unhappy event would cause. I was touched by his generosity, but it gave me the bitterest feelings I had ever experienced in my life, to find myself considered an object of compassion.

I had no friends in Paris ; my money was nearly gone, and the necessity of taking some immediate steps towards home, would not allow me to give way to the bitterness of my grief. I had not sufficient money to pay for a passage from Havre to New-York, and I could not think of asking credit, with a probability of being unable to pay on my arrival. In looking over a file of English papers at Galignani's the day before, I had seen in Gore's Advertiser, the ship Seneca advertised to sail in a few days from Liverpool for New-York. This ship belonged to the merchants in whose counting-room I had served my time ; I was well acquainted with the master, and I determined to return to England immediately, and go home in her ; for I knew that a passage would cost me nothing. I left Paris the next morning, and arrived at Liverpool in three days. But a new disappointment awaited me. The Seneca had hauled out of dock, was still in sight, and bound down the river. The wind and tide were in her favour, and I found it would be impossible to overtake her with a boat. I returned to the Star and Garter Hotel in Castle-street, where I had landed, in a most unhappy state of mind. The expenses of coming from Paris had left me with a

2

bare sovereign, but little more than enough to de-
fray another day's expenses at the hotel.

I had but little time for thought; the next packet
for New-York would not leave under a week, and
even though I should get credit for a passage, what
would support me in the mean time ?   I could sell
my watch.   But it was a gift from my father ; and
I could not endure the thought of parting with it.
I could go as a steerage passenger ; but I had no
money to purchase provisions ; and I remembered
how wretchedly the steerage passengers had seemed to live on board the Philadelphia, how they were
abused by the mate, and jeered by the sailors ; my
soul revolted at the thought of herding with such
people.   By appealing to some of the American
ship-masters in the port, I could doubtless have bor-
rowed the money ; but as I had no prospect of re-
paying it when I got home, I could not entertain
such an idea.   It was humiliating enough to return
to my mother penniless ; I would not go to her in
debt.   Could I work my passage ?   The thing seemed impossible, but why should I not ?   why should
not I work as well as another ?   was I composed of
more precious material than other men ?   If not,
why should I be exempt from their toils and hardships ?   The possibility of such a thing gave me
new life, and I went to bed and slept more soundly
than I had done since I heard of my father's death.
I rose early in the morning, paid for my lodging, for
I had not ventured to eat anything at the hotel, told
the clerk that I would send an order for my baggage, and sallied out, resolutely bent on looking
steadily at Fortune, let her frown upon me as harsh-
ly as she might.

It was the last day of November ; a cold, dreary,
drizzling day ; a dirty yellowish vapour hung over
the city, so impervious to the sun's rays, that from
any luminous appearance in the sky it was impossi-

ble to determine in what quarter of the heavens
the great illuminator of our globe was shedding his
beams. A suffocating stench of coal smoke per-
vaded the atmosphere, and everything dripped,
dripped, dripped, dismally with rain; the gutters
poured out never-failing streams of muddy water,
too thick and slow to make a bubble; most of the
shops had gas lights burning; and the fish-women,
with baskets of herrings upon their heads, as they
waded their miserable rounds, seemed too disheartened to cry their scaly commodities. Everybody
was encased in oil-cloth, as though rain was a matter of course, quite the natural order of things; and
women stalked securely through the streets with
high pattens on their feet, which showed that long
practice had enabled them to walk securely on those
dangerous-looking stilts. Heavy, dismal, cheerless.
I wonder now that I had the heart, in such an atmosphere, to keep my resolve. One such a day in
New-York would create a panic, but here it was a
matter of course. If it produced any effect at all,
it only caused a trifling increase in the consumption
of ale. If a traveller were to enter Liverpool on a
clear day, he would be likely to notice the great
number of " ale and spirit vaults," sooner than anything else; but on a day like this he would not think
there was one too many; although nearly every
other house in the business parts of the town dis-
plays either a bunch of grapes, or an " arms" of
some kind.

Travellers pretend to discover a resemblance in
Liverpool to New-York; but the likeness is such as
that of Monmouth to Macedon; there's a river runs
by New-York, and there's a river runs by Liverpool,—but here all likeness ends. There are not
two places in the world more unlike.

Having made a cheap breakfast at a gloomy chop-
house in Pool Lane, I went directly to a second-hand

clothing dealer's in Dale-street, and exchanged the clothes I had on for a complete suit of thick sea-togs, including a varnished sou'wester, a canvass cap lined with flannel, fitting tight to the head, the hinder part of it forming a kind of cape for the shoulders to keep the rain from running down the neck. My clothes were nearly new, so I received ten shillings besides the sea-togs, which, added to the remains of my last sovereign, gave me seventeen shillings ; quite a little fortune, it seemed to me, now that I had got on a covering which I was not taxed for the privilege of wearing.

# CHAPTER III.

## THE SCATTERGOOD.

I FELT very sailorish, but a professional observer would have detected some little incongruities between my manner and my dress, which would have revealed the fulness of my pretensions to the character I had assumed. It would be easier to ape the port of an emperor than the gait of a sailor. Of all the shams in the world there is none so easily detected as a sham sailor. However, regardless of the rain and the cold, the dismal lowering clouds, and drooping tendency that seemed to possess everything, I moved briskly through the dirty lanes and alleys that conducted me to Prince's Dock, where the majority of the American ships in port lay. I went the rounds of the dock, applying to every ship I found bound home, first for a berth as a sailor, and then for the privilege of working my passage. I was on the point of abandoning the pursuit in despair, when I espied a little dirty-looking bark with a high poop, which I had at first taken for an Englishman, with Baltimore painted on her quarter boards. Her name was the Scattergood, and a full length figure of her patronymic decorated her cutwater.

Unlike all the other American ships in the dock, she was a very shabby, disorderly-looking craft: her rigging all hanging in bights, points and gaskets flying from her yards, and her side and bulwarks stained with iron rust, she looked as though she had been fitted out by the parish. Her decks were in confusion, and her mates looked like anything but

2*

sailors. I stepped on board and asked for the captain ; the cook, a Chinaman, pointed him out to me, standing upon the poop. He was a feeble little old man, dressed in a long snuff-coloured surtout ; his hands were encased in a pair of buckskin mittens, and he was trying to screen himself from the penetrating mist by holding a faded green cotton umbrella over his head. The ship, her master, and her crew, seemed made for each other. But I was not in a condition to be squeamish ; so without taking a very critical view of the wretched craft, I asked the captain to ship me as a sailor. He replied in a querulous piping voice, " No, no, no, I wont. I don't want you. What's your name ?" I told him. " Go ashore, go ashore, go ashore, I wont have you."

To be driven off by such a character rather touched my pride, and I meant he should have me. So paying no attention to him, I told him he would miss it if he didn't take me.

"I wont have you, I can't, I can't, I don't like your looks ; get out of my way, I don't want you."

So far from being intimidated by this unhandsome repulse, I felt angry with the miserable old skipper, and resolved he should have me. " If you wont give me wages," I said, " I will go without pay ; but you must take me ; I want to get home to my friends."

" What's your name ?" I told him again.

" Are you a good sailor ?"

" No, I am no sailor at all."

" I wont have you. You'll eat too much."

" Shall I go with you ?" I said again, pretending not to hear his last reply.

" Plague on you, yes ; if you will only leave me. The bark will sail after dinner, so bring your kit right off."

" Thank you, thank you," I replied, and jumping ashore, I ran to the hotel where I had left my baggage, and delivering an order for it which I had written myself, the porter gave me my trunk and carpet-bag, without recognising me, and I took them upon my back and bore them off to the bark, where I stowed them away in the forecastle; very strange looking baggage for a sailor. The forecastle was a wretched hole. It was even with the ship's deck, a mere shelter from the rain, called a top-gallant forecastle. The berths were merely rough boards loosely nailed together; and as the chain-cables led directly through it, warmth and comfort were utter impossibilities, for the hawse-holes would admit water in all weathers, when there was the least motion to the ship, and the bulk-head was too slight and rickety to keep out the wind. It was not a very encouraging prospect for a winter passage across the Atlantic, particularly for me, as I had but a scanty supply of sea-clothing; but I was not disheartened by it. Anything seemed better than getting in debt. Besides, I should have companions, and I had too much pride to shrink from anything which more experienced men made no hesitation in encountering. It appeared, however, that the ship's whole crew had run away on account of this very top-gallant forecastle, and a new crew had been shipped, who shook their heads and looked very dismal when they saw what accommodations they had got to put up with. However, it was too late for repentance, they had received their month's advance, and were forced to go, but they looked very grum about it. When all the sailors were on board, the dock-gates were opened, lines were run out, and we began to warp the bark out into the stream. I worked as hard as I could, kept falling over ropes, and hauling upon everything, and raised dreadful blisters upon my hands. The two mates flew about from one part of the ship to the other, made a tremendous noise, were cursed by the pilot.

and shook their fists at the dock-gate men, who laughed at them, and called them Yankees. The wretched little captain stood all the while in a bewildered state, holding his cotton umbrella over his head, on the poop-deck, seemingly quite unconscious where the ship was going, or what they were doing with her. The sailors in the midst of all manned the capstan, and began to sing a merry air with a roaring chorus, ending in "Round the rock to Sally."

The two mates were as great curiosities in their way as the skipper himself. They were brothers; one of them wore a bob-tailed pepper and salt coat, with steel buttons, such as the flashy grocers in Orange and Mulberry streets wear when they go down town to buy cheap goods at auction, and the other, the second mate, sported a blue embroidered jacket, with large frogs, such as the skippers of Havanna and Mexican traders wear in New-Orleans. After an inconceivable waste of noise and ill-directed exertion, the Scattergood got fairly into the stream, the sails were loosened and sheeted home, a fair breeze sprung up, the heavy yellow clouds which had been all the morning hanging over the city began to loosen and melt away, and just as we rounded Black-Rock, the sun, which was fast sinking to the horizon, suddenly burst out, and illumined our ship with a ray of cheerful light that was quite electrifying. I was very willing to receive it as a happy augury, for I had need of something to keep my spirits from falling to zero.

The little breeze that had sprung up when we first quitted the dock, died away soon after the sun went down, the clouds all disappeared, and as it grew dark, the stars began to glitter and shine as we lay becalmed the whole night. And a mercy it was, for such was the want of order and regularity on board, that had it chanced to blow hard, we must have gone to the bottom. It being very still, gave us in the forecastle an opportunity to make the most of our accommodations. Wretched as they were, my companions did not appear to regard them as unusual, from which I supposed they had lived in as uncomfortable quarters before, and if they had not found them supportable, would never have sought such again ; and I took heart, determined not to repine at what others could endure with cheerfulness, although it seemed to me impossible that I could ever live, even for one passage across the Atlantic, in such a hole.

It was quite dark before we were ordered to go to our supper, and as the watches had not been chosen, all hands went into the forecastle, excepting only the man at the wheel, (the helmsman.) A tub of boiled salt beef, very salt and very hard, resembling a knotty piece of mahogany, and another tub of navy bread, biscuits made of wheaten bran, called middlings, were brought to us by the cook, who informed us that no small stores, tea, coffee and molasses, were allowed. Some of the sailors grumbled a little at this information, and asked for a light, and the steward brought word from the captain that no light would be allowed. This caused a more general murmur of discontent, but one of the sailors had brought a pound of candles on board in his chest, and he lighted one and stuck it in an empty porter bottle that we had found in the forecastle, and good humour soon prevailed among us. The sailors' chests served for seats, and we arranged ourselves in a very small circle, with the beef and bread in the centre, and helped ourselves in turn, the oldest sailor taking the piece of beef in his hands first, and passing it round. I had eaten nothing since morning, and I had a voracious appetite ; repulsive as this manner of carving seemed to me, I was rather impatient for my turn at the kid. I believe I ate my share of the bread and beef, although I could not help contrasting this meal with my last on shore, and thinking of Mivart's and the Star and Garter. I am not certain that I ever enjoyed one better. It was the first bread and meat that I had ever eaten in the sweat of my own brow. One of the crew had brought on board a small jug of beer, for rum was too costly a drink to be indulged in, which he served out to us, reserving no larger share for himself than he gave to the others. There was a fraternal kindness in this little act, that impressed me very favourably towards my shipmates. A jug of beer is no great matter on shore, but at the outset of a winter passage across the Atlantic, in a ship where no drops of comfort of any kind could be looked for, but a great many of cold water were certain, it required a degree of generosity amounting almost to heroism, to enable one to share such a precious cordial with others. The generous fellow who dealt out his beer so freely, proved to be one of the most chivalrous souls I have ever known. In the little time that we were together, I witnessed so many acts of true heroism in him, actions performed in the dark, when he was not conscious of being seen, that I have ever entertained a high regard for his memory. He called himself Jack Plasket, though I found afterwards it was an assumed name. He was young, exceedingly good-looking, and though a thorough sailor, well educated, and evidently accustomed to the society of very different associates from his present forecastle companions. There was a mystery about him which I could not unravel. He was rather an exception to, than a specimen of, the sailor character. But disinterestedness is by no means a rare virtue in the forecastle.

Another thing that pleased me among my rude companions, was their cutting off the best piece of beef and putting it aside for their absent companion —the man at the wheel. I found that sailors were

very exact in the performance of certain little
punctilios in their conduct towards each other, and
that they regarded a breach of their code of sea
morals with superstitious fear. I heard one relate
a story of a shipmate who once called the watch ten
minutes too soon, and the next night fell from aloft
and was drowned; a judgment that he seemed to
consider neither doubtful, nor disproportioned to the
offence.

The hardships of sailors are so unmixed with
pleasures; their sufferings are so certain, and their
deprivations so much a matter of course, that they
can never afford to look upon the dark side of their
circumstances. If they should once stop to think,
they would be lost; nothing but the most determined cheerfulness can ever keep them in heart.
When they do murmur, it is about the most incon-
siderable trifles, as if they did it to keep their thoughts
from dwelling on their real grievances.

When our supper was finished, instead of indulging in gloomy anticipations, or of wasting any idle
regrets over their past days of joviality, they blew
out the candle, with a praiseworthy spirit of econo-
my, and began to sing a dismal ballad with a chorus. It is a great mistake to suppose that vulgar
people have vulgar tastes; at least the uneducated
vulgar. They are always fond of sentiment. The
popular forecastle ditties might be sung by a choir
of nuns. There are a few boisterous songs that
have found their way to the forecastle, but they are
rather tolerated than admired, and I have noticed
that sailors alway listen to them with a very apparent disrelish; but when the ballad is long drawn
out, with the sufferings of some distressed damsel, if
a princess all the better, or the miseries of some de-
spairing cavalier, they will sit like children listening
to the witch stories of an old beldame; and the sad
strain seems to touch a responsive chord in every

bosom. Dibdin's sea songs are very admirable for nautical dramas, but they are as ill adapted to the forecastle as Italian bravuras are for real lovers. A genuine sea song never contains any nautical slang; that would be homely and common-place; but in the theatre it satisfies the sentiment; for sentiment can only endure what is foreign.

Our songs did not last long, for the mate came to the door of the forecastle and mustered us all upon deck to choose watches. There were twelve of us, and the chief mate had his first choice of men. The second mate represents the captain, and makes the second selection. They chose a man alternately, and by this means the good and bad are equally distributed in the two watches. The first man chosen was Jack Plaskett, and the mate showed his discrimination in selecting him; but his superiority was so obvious that he would have been a dolt not to have done so. Fortunately for me, I got in the mate's watch, for I was anxious to be put in the same watch with Jack. As I had brought no bed on board, not knowing that bedding was not provided by the ship, I was obliged to ask one of the other watch to allow me the privilege of sleeping in his berth when he was on deck. I met with no difficulty in finding somebody who allowed me this privilege, and I turned in at eight o'clock and slept soundly till twelve, when we were called up to let the other watch turn in. It was not very pleasant to turn out of a warm berth and stand four hours on deck; but the night being calm, though cold, I soon coiled myself on deck and fell asleep; but I woke before the watch had half expired, almost dead with cold. The wind had changed again, and we were enveloped in sleet, the decks were slippery, and the motion of the ship being quick and jerking, owing partly to the short waves caused by the current running opposite to the wind, and partly to the dead weight of our cargo, it was with great difficulty that I could stand upon my feet. My hands were blistered and cracked, and the salt water, though it probably had a healing effect, yet gave me indescribable pain. There was a good deal of work above and aloft, but I could only haul upon a rope when it was put into my hands, for I could neither understand the orders that were given, nor execute them when explained to me. At four o'clock the starboard watch was called, and we again turned in, but I was so wet and cold, and my hands were so painful, that I found it impossible to sleep ; and I was not sorry when the watch was again called at half-past seven to turn out. We were called half an hour before the watch had expired, to give us time to get breakfast, that the other watch might have their full time below. Or at least this is the general practice, but in this case the other watch was not allowed to turn in after breakfast, as it was necessary for all hands to work in putting the ship in order while she was in the channel. Our breakfast consisted only of the remains of the dry piece of indigestible beef that had served for our suppers, and a bit of hard bread. I thought it hard fare, and when I saw the steward taking the cabin breakfast aft, consisting of hot coffee and boiled potatoes, I blushed to find myself following the smoking dish of humble vegetables with a lickerish eye.

About nine o'clock we discharged our pilot off Point Linus. There was too high a sea running to allow the small boat to be lowered, and they threw a rope from the pilot boat, which the pilot fastened under his arms in a bowline, leaped overboard, and in that manner was drawn on board his boat ; as the two vessels neared each other, the cook threw on board the pilot boat a piece of salt beef. This I found was the custom when a pilot is taken on board or discharged. All hands were now set to work, seizing on scotchmen, that is, fastening long strips of board upon the stays and rigging, where they come in contact with the ship's yards, to prevent chafing ; so that a ship at sea looks as though she had been wounded in her rigging, and all the sore places had bandages upon them. This was simple work, and I had no very great difficulty in doing my part; but when I first went aloft I could not work with that feeling of security which comes to one after a little practice ; my head swam when I looked down upon deck, and twice I came near falling ; and my sickness increased when I went to mast-head, but I found that continual exercise helped to cure me. The sailors soon discerned my greenness, but were very patient in explaining the names and uses of the ropes, and in teaching me the art of making knots.

The wind was ahead, the fog was very dense, and in consequence of the narrowness of the channel, we were compelled to tack the ship every two hours, which kept us very busy, and my arms were so cramped and lame from continued hauling, it was painful to lift my hand above my head. As night approached the wind increased, and we were forced to shorten sail to close-reefed topsails and a reefed foresail and jib.

Our miserable little captain walked back and forth in front of the poop, with his hands behind him, looking pale and frightened, and every now and then called one of his mates to him and asked him what he thought about it. It was plain enough that the captain thought it a very doubtful prospect. The only man on board excepting the officers, who had left home in the ship, was a Dutch carpenter, who informed us that this was the captain's first voyage. I was sufficiently startled at this, but much more so when he said that our captain was a tailor ; that six months before he commanded a clothing-store in

Philadelphia : but with a hope of improving his health and his fortune, he had sold out his establishment and bought this old ship, worn out in the Canton trade, and had shipped the two brothers now on board for his navigators ; obtained a freight for Liverpool in Savannah, and was now returning with a load of salt for Philadelphia. The ship was leaky, her rigging was rotten, and her sails old ; and to increase the catalogue of our mischances, the mates were in the habit of indulging in too strong potations of brandy. A knowledge of our condition had a disheartening effect on the crew, for they were all old sailors, who knew the dangers of the channel, and the rough time we should have of it on our passage across the Atlantic. While a sailor can have confidence in his officers, he dismisses all care for himself, knowing that there is somebody who will neglect nothing essential to his safety ; but joviality loves not the companionship of care, and I found that sailors could be serious and thoughtful, like their betters, when they felt that self-preservation depended upon their own exertions.

Instead of songs and long yarns, when we went into the forecastle, the watch debated the chances of our getting safe out of the channel ; every one had some dismal tale to tell of shipwreck and danger. One of the watch was a native of the Isle of Man, and his intimate knowledge of the reefs and shoals in that part of the channel where we now were, added to his apprehension, and many a frightful story did he tell us of shipwrecks about the coast, which he had witnessed when a boy. The mates had never been in the channel before, one of them having been always employed in the Canton trade, and the other had only been in the coasting service.

We kept constantly tacking during the night, and once we narrowly escaped plumping upon a reef of rocks, called the Calf of Man. The fog was thick;

and suddenly a light flashed on our deck from the leeward; the man on the look out cried out " breakers,
breakers, put down your helm !" The watch jumped
out upon deck, for they had not undressed themselves, but lay down in their wet clothes on their
chests, and we succeeded in getting the ship headed
round on the other tack. The light seemed close
aboard of us, and it could not have been far off, or
we could not have seen it through the fog. At daylight the fog lifted a little, like a curtain, just to
show us the Welsh coast under our lee, and then
shut down again, more dense and impenetrable than
ever. The wind continuing to blow, we were not
able to make any sail, so we drifted back towards
the Isle of Man again, and continued to tack every
two hours during the day. Excitement and hard
work together, had entirely cured my sea-sickness,
and I began to feel myself of some consequence. I
could run about deck without falling, and go to any
rope in the dark that I was ordered to; it still made
me dizzy to go aloft, but soon this feeling began to
wear off. The wind and the fog continued, and
some of the sailors said they had known such weather
to last in the channel more than a month. We began
to calculate the chances of escape in the forecastle,
in the event of the ship getting ashore, and the most
experienced among us agreed that they were very
slender. The sailors tied up their little valuables in
handkerchiefs, to be prepared for quitting the ship at
a moment's warning, for the ignorance of our officers
was now apparent, and we had very nearly the
command of the vessel ; the man at the wheel taking
it upon himself to tell the captain when it was time
to tack the ship.

Nothing was further from my thoughts than a wish
to create dissatisfaction among the crew, but I
thought it would be a wicked deference to the
captain of the ship, merely because he was our su-

perior in office, to allow him to peril our lives and
the safety of his ship, without remonstrating with
him, and I told the crew that it was their duty to
advise him to put back to Liverpool, and provide
himself with suitable officers and a new suit of sails,
before he attempted to cross the Atlantic.   The majority of them shook their heads at the proposition,
for they said it could be construed as mutiny; but
Jack Plaskett was in favour of the measure, and
offered to stand by me if I would make a move.
But seeing that I was the youngest man in the forecastle, and only a green hand, I thought it would
be rather a bold step, and declined, unless they
would all go aft with me.   This they refused to do,
and we had another fearful night.   The next day
our little captain appeared quite bewildered and beside himself; the mates were half drunk, and
acknowledged that neither they nor the captain
knew where the ship was.   The storm continued
without abatement, and at four o'clock in the afternoon, I discovered a very high bluff through the fog
at the leeward, and ran aft and told the captain
that there was land under our lee.   " I know it,"
he replied.   " Do you know what land it is ?" I
said.   " Yes, it's Bluemorris."   " No," I said, " it is
not Beaumaris ; we are on the opposite side of the
channel ; this is either the coast of Lancashire or
Ireland ; and if you don't put the ship about, we
shall be ashore in a few minutes."   " Do you think
so ?" he said, looking very much terrified, " then tell
the mate to 'bout ship."

By the time the ship was put upon the other tack,
we were very close in shore, and the land was so
distinctly visible, that our Manxman in the forecastle knew it to be St. Bee's head.   A very few
minutes longer, and we should have been ashore.
The wind increased as the sun went down, and we
reefed the foresail, took in the jib, and close-reefed

the spanker. The mates, seeing that the captain was frightened, grew frightened themselves, and drank so much brandy that they were soon stupidly drunk ; the captain retired to his cabin and locked himself in, and then there was no officer upon deck. The storm continued to increase, the wind drew more to the north, and· the fog turned to hail. I now told the men that there was no other course left for us but to take charge of the ship, and try to preserve her until morning, and then advise the captain to return to Liverpool, and if he should hesitate, to compel him. They agreed to be governed by my advice. But I was entirely incapable of giving any in regard to the management of the ship, and as none of us knew anything about the tides or the depth of water, or the proper course to be steered, I told the carpenter, if he would go to the captain's cabin and get his chart and navigator, I would try to prick off our course ; for I had learned something about navigation at school, and the captain of the Philadelphia, in our passage to London, had taught me how to mark a ship's position on the chart. The captain had locked himself in his stateroom, and the only way we could get at his chart was by forcing the lid off his chest. This the carpenter did, and by the aid of a pair of dividers and a ruler, I found that we were a few miles southeast of St. Bee's head, on the coast of Lancashire, and that the tide was drifting us directly on shore. I called Jack Plaskett, and told him our situation ; and he said that the only way of saving the ship would be to make more sail, but he was afraid of carrying away the spars if we did so. We held a consultation with the rest of the crew, and it was at last determined to make sail. We accordingly shook a reef out of the foresail, hoisted the jib, loosed the mainsail, and then set the spanker. As we got aboard the main tack, and flattened in the jib sheet,

the increased force of the wind caused the ship to
leap and plunge like a spirited horse when the whip
is applied to his back. The masts bent like a pop-
lar tree in a nor'wester, and every time she plunged
into the waves, I thought they would all have gone
by the board. Every man was on deck, ready to
execute an order the moment it was given ; and the
carpenter stood at the mainmast with an axe in his
hand, to cut away the masts if we should strike the
bottom ; the long-boat was got ready for hoisting
out; and the lead was kept going, to find out whether
we shoaled the water. As I was the least efficient
hand on deck, I stationed myself on the foretopsail-
yard, to look out for breakers, but the cold was so
intense that I could not remain long. Not one of
the crew lay down for the night, and by morning we were all pretty well exhausted ; but as day
was breaking, the captain and mate both came on
deck. It was time to tack ship, for I judged we
were well over upon the Welsh coast, as it proved we
were when it grew lighter, and I told the captain he
had better put the ship about. He gave orders to
the mate to do so, and we wore round. The wind
had moderated a little, and the ship laboured less
than she had during the night; but the press of canvass that she was still under, made it rather unsafe
and uncomfortable to stand upon deck.

It was now certain that we should have another
such a night as the last, and perhaps a worse one,
unless we carried our resolution into effect, and
compelled the captain to put back. The crew were
faint-hearted, but I called them together and told
them they had nothing to fear ; that the captain
would be ashamed to make any complaint against
us, and that if he did so, we could easily prove by
the carpenter and steward, that but for our exertions the ship would have been lost ; and instead of
blame, they would get the thanks of the insurers, at

least. I tried to prevail upon the oldest sailor to be spokesman for us, but he urged that he had no gift of speaking; and as they all said that I could do it best, I consented, very unwillingly, to take the lead, knowing that if any difficulty should ensue, that I would be singled out as the ringleader. I accordingly marched aft to the cabin-door, with all the crew at my back, and asked for the captain. The mates turned pale as they saw us coming, and retreated into their hurricane-house, and the captain came out trembling, and asked what we wanted.

I represented to him that the crew were unwilling to continue the voyage, unless the ship were better supplied with sails; and that it was their opinion, his proper course would be to square his yards and go back to Liverpool, and wait for a fair wind, before he ventured out to sea again. Two or three of the sailors spoke up, and said they thought so too. The captain looked very much puzzled, but ruminating a minute or two, he said he thought we were about half right, called out for the mate, and told him to square the yards and go back into port. I was rejoiced to hear this, for I was fearful of being compelled to speak in a harsher manner; and we all went to work shaking reefs out of the topsails, and making sail,—for as soon as we began to sail before the wind, it seemed comparatively light. By ten o'clock we were opposite Point Linus, where we took another pilot, and that evening, at dusk, we dropped anchor opposite George's Dock, in Liverpool. As I had neither signed the ship's papers, nor taken any advance wages, I had a right to leave the ship when I pleased, and I made up my mind to do so without delay, and to take the precaution of inquiring whether the captain of any other ship I could get on board of were a tailor or a sailor, before I went to sea again. My shipmates looked upon me as a hero, and said that if I left the bark, they would not remain behind. A wherry came off from the shore, and they bargained with the boatman to come back at midnight with a larger boat to take us all from the ship. It chanced to be a clear starry night, and one of the mates kept watch to prevent the desertion of the crew. The boat was rowed a long distance above the ship, and then dropped down directly in range of her bows, so that she could not be seen from the poop, where the mate was walking. We all passed our dunnage, chests and hammocks, over the bow without being discovered, and then jumped into the boat, and shoved off, leaving only the cook and steward behind. I felt very happy to be free from such an uncomfortable and dangerous craft; and now that I knew what I could endure in the way of work and hard fare, I felt much better prepared to take the rough side of things, than I did before I had been tried. As I was a stranger in Liverpool, I was compelled to follow my shipmates after we got ashore to their boarding-house, at the sign of the Ship in Old Hall-street, where they spent the remainder of the night in drinking ale, smoking, and singing. I had some fear of difficulty with the little tailor captain, and to keep out of his reach, I went to live with an acquaintance of Mrs. Collins, the landlady of the Ship, who occupied a cellar near the Clarence Dock, and supported herself by washing for sailors. Her husband was a Swede, who occasionally earned a trifle as a ship-keeper. Their entire establishment consisted of two very small rooms in the cellar of a new brick house, the upper part of which was occupied by people in the higher walks of life, as was very proper; two families—one the family of a ship-joiner, and the other a blockmaker. Of course, we in the cellar had no communication with those so much above us. My hostess was an excellent woman,—devout, neat, cheerful;

her husband was a quiet, intelligent man, and unaf-
fectedly pious. In the evening, when her work was
done, and her hearth cleanly swept, one or two of
her gossips would drop in with their sewing, generally some part of a sailor's wardrobe, for it was a
marine neighbourhood, and I used to listen to their
conversation with pleasure and profit. One woman
interested me above all the others. She was a meek,
gentle creature, whose husband belonged to a fish-
ing smack ; she busied herself all the time of his ab-
sence, in mending his clothes, and selling the fish
that he brought ; and he repaid her by spending his
earnings at the ale-house, and beating her when he
came home to her drunk. This I learned from one
of her cronies, for she made no complaints of the
brute herself, but when spoken to about her husband,
she would look as cheerful as she could, and say,
"James is doing pretty well, but he will do better
one of these days."

Mr. and Mrs. Peterson, my host and hostess, indulged in the luxury of meat only on Sundays ; at
other times, bread and butter formed the staple of
our meals ; and Saturday night was quite a gala
night with them, for then, in company with some of
their neighbours, they went to St. George's Market,
and after promenading through long avenues of
vegetables, game, poultry and fruits, and pricing
rounds of beef, saddles of venison, cauliflowers and
oranges, they would come home bringing a small
bit of beef in a very large covered basket ; and the
price of provisions furnished a topic of conversation
until the recurrence of another Saturday night. I
never expected to regard a piece of baked beef and
potatoes as a very grand affair, but it was impossible
to sit down with these honest people to their Sunday dinner without sympathizing with their feelings.
The meat was salted and dredged with flour over
night, all ready for the oven, to avoid unnecessary

work on Sunday morning, and placed upon a high shelf; and covered with a snowy white napkin. In the morning Peterson took it to the baker's with an air bordering on grandeur; holding his head higher than on ordinary occasions, for he had a drooping habit on other days, as though he had no right to carry his head erect. But when he brought it home —that was the most trying time, for all house-keepers know that beef will shrink in baking, if not killed in the right quarter of the moon, and to people who eat beef but once a week, it is a matter of intense curiosity whether their joint has shrunk or swollen in the oven.

"I don't think it has shrunk much, Peterson," the cheerful creature would say, as she looked anxiously at the pan when Peterson placed it upon the table.

"Shrunk! no, I believe, as I am living, it is greater as ever," the hopeful Peterson would reply, smacking his lips as he looked at the unusual luxury.

"At all events, there's plenty of gravy, and the potatoes are browned very nice," said Mrs. Peterson.

"They are lovely; I don't believe as the king has got better spuds for dinner as them," responded her husband.

The little deal table was spread with very humble appointments, but in the purity of neatness, and when we took our seats, Mrs. Peterson asked a blessing, a longer one than usual, not only because the dinner was better, but to prolong the enjoyment and make the most of it. Mrs. Peterson not only said grace, but she carved, her husband being inexpert with the knife, and made an imposing ceremony of it. First, the knife must be deliberately sharpened; then its edge must be felt; then the fork must be thrust into the beef, and a little time taken up in observing whether the juice were red or not; then the joint must be properly placed in the dish, and after a preliminary flourish with the knife, the first slice is cut; rich, juicy, and altogether delightful; quite beyond the suspicion of a fault. It is necessary to eat baked beef and potatoes under such circumstances, to comprehend their merits; and so eaten, they are finer, more digestible and healthier, than any fricandeau that ever came from the hands of a Parisian cook. Mrs. Peterson was not entirely free from human weaknesses, and with a vanity that none but a very pious person could condemn, she informed me that she and Peterson had often had a gooseberry tart for dinner in the summer when fruit was plenty, and that once they had been the owners of quite a large basket of American apples, which were presented to them by the *sthuard* of a liner. And the fragrant recollections of these rarities served a long while for a dessert after dinner; and it gave me greater pleasure to hear her tell of them than it would to have partaken of them.

It was impossible to remain long in the society of Mr. and Mrs. Peterson (by the way, nobody but myself ever applied the Mr. to Peterson's name,) without feeling conscious that the hearts of these good people must be buoyed up by the recollection of some departed glory which had once surrounded them. There was a mysterious dignity, a solemn content, which seemed to envelope them, as though they were not what they seemed, but were willing that the world should regard them as a childless couple, living happily on four shillings a week; only, if the world did but know something which they knew themselves! Such an air the rebel duke of Berwick must have had, when he used to sit with his peasant wife in the company of his rude neighbours, who never suspected him of being better than themselves, except in manners; and so Louis Philippe must have seemed, when he earned his bread by teaching a school. I had partly made up my mind that Peterson was, at the least, a descendant of Gustavus Vasa, when the secret of their quiet dignity leaked out. Their fire-side had once been blessed by the presence of an angel, a little boy-angel, a child of their own, who was too bright, too beautiful for this world, and had been taken home to Heaven. Little Frederick! There never was such a child; everybody said so, even Mrs. Briton, the baker's wife. It was foreseen from the first that the child would never live to grow up; Peterson, himself, who of course knew the child thoroughly, said more than a hundred times, "that child is too knowing to live." The child died before it reached its first birth day, and yet, would anybody believe that there could be people in the world of a nature so depraved as to doubt, nay, even to positively say, that there never had been such a child; that little Frederick was a humbug? To the disgrace of humanity, it cannot be denied there were such people; and to the disgrace of the female sex, it must be owned that one such person was a lady, Mrs. Barker, the wife of another ship-keeper, who had never had any children of her own, and was unwilling that any of her neighbours should have the advantage of her in that respect. But there were little Frederick's shoes, as genuine a pair of dear little shoes as ever were worn upon a baby's feet, and there was the cradle, and the spoon, and the little cups. How could anybody refuse to believe in little Frederick? For my own part, I believe in little Frederick as firmly as I do in any of my creditors, and were it not for my sins, I should expect to meet him in Heaven.

In the family of the ship-joiner above our heads, lived, as a servant, a pretty black-eyed Jewess. Her name was Antoinette; her family name I have

forgotten. Her father was a wealthy jeweller, with
a house at Everton, and she had been turned out
of doors for joining the established church; and
having received but an indifferent education, and
being shunned by all her tribe, she had been compelled to go to service for a livelihood. She, too,
was an occasional visiter in Mrs. Peterson's cellar,
and her black eyes and rosy lips gave a tinge of romance to the homely scene; for Mrs. Peterson herself was a plain woman, as were all her cronies, the
brightness of their womanhood having faded, or
rather lost its glossiness of surface, and like a
piece of good cloth, showed the fineness of the
material of which it was composed the better for
it. And here the pretty Christianized Jewess
and Jack Plaskett met one evening by accident,
and fell in love with each other directly. He
was too honourable to marry her and leave her to
toil in a kitchen, and she loved him too well to let
him leave her; so, like a fond Jessica, she proposed
to put on the habit of a sailor and follow him to sea.
But he would not consent to it, knowing, as she did
not, the perils and hardships of a sailor's life. Although her father had turned her from his doors,
and would allow neither her brothers nor sisters to
afford her any relief, she loved them still, and used to
make them stealthy visits by night, always creeping
like a menial into the kitchen door of her father's
house. Once I accompanied her there with Jack
Plaskett, and we stopped at the corner of the street,
while she went in alone. It was a handsome house,
with a large garden in the rear, and from the appearance of numerous lights and the bustle of ser-
vants, I supposed they must be entertaining company. She was gone but a few minutes, and returned
to us weeping. She refused to tell what had happened, but I heard afterwards that she had encountered her father in the garden, and that he took her

by the arm and thrust her rudely into the street. I know not whether her family were ever reconciled to her; and as Jack Plaskett was drowned on his next voyage, I fear that poor Antoinette is still a patient drudge in some humble kitchen. Perhaps she is in Heaven.

The Scattergood lay in the river but three or four days, and then sailed with a fair wind and a new crew. I believe she reached Philadelphia that voyage, but was wrecked the next. As soon as she was fairly under way, I left my troglodytish lodging and rose into the upper air; and after much trouble, succeeded in getting a berth on board a New-York liner, the name of which I must omit, lest I give offence to somebody in the course of my little narrative. She was a new ship, I believe it was only her second voyage, well equipped, strongly manned, a fast sailer, and a perfect beauty to look at. She was the handsomest vessel in port. Everything about her was neat, substantial, and in perfect order. She had a flush deck, as smooth as a nine-pin alley, varnished waists, which looked like a strip of yellow satin, and a gilded billet-head, with scroll-work, copied from some of Raphael's frescoes, for it was before poop-decks, painted ports, and figure-heads had come in fashion. There were three mates, two stewards, two cooks, twenty sailors, two boys, and a carpenter. We hauled out of dock on the 14th of December, and in three days were out of the channel and past Cape Clear. The weather was cold and murky, the nights were long and dreary, but our officers were experienced, the ship was new, and I had a home in prospect, so I looked resolutely ahead, and strove to forget my present discomforts by imagining future pleasures.

Our forecastle was a handsome apartment compared with the wretched top-gallant forecastle of the Scattergood. Our fare, too, was comparatively

sumptuous; a tin pot full of tea every night and
morning, sweetened with Cuba molasses; it was
not exactly pecco, but it was hot, and quite as whole-
some as Oulong Souchong; and the weather being
very cold, even the hot steam was refreshing.   In
addition to this luxury, we were served twice a week
with a kid of lob-skous, a hash of salt meat and potatoes, seasoned with a dash of hot water, which
made it very acceptable, after we had worked hard
in the wet and cold all night.   And then we had the
very great luxury of a tub of hot mush and molasses
occasionally, very nearly, but not quite so good as
that which is given to criminals in our city prison.
I do not mean, by this comparison, to intimate that
we were entitled to as good fare as prisoners, because they are frequently gentlemen, who have been
used to better times, and of course are entitled to
more consideration than mere sailors, who are generally treated as though they were entitled to nothing but hard work and hard words.

We had the same labour to perform on board the
liner the first few days after leaving port, that we
had on board the Scattergood; for it is the practice
on board of all ships, to strip their rigging and spars
of all superfluous gear, when lying in the dock, to
give them an appearance of neatness and order.
But as we had more men in proportion to the size
of our ship, our work was sooner finished, and we
were indulged with watch-and-watch,—four hours
on deck, and four hours below, night and day, excepting when we were making or taking in sail;
and then all hands were kept at work.   It is the
custom on board of packet ships, to carry sail as
long as possible, and often when they do attempt to
take it in, they are obliged to let it go altogether.
It sometimes happens that the officer on deck is not
possessed of sufficient judgment to know when to
take in and when to make sail, and thereby the

greater part of those disasters at sea, which we read of in the papers, take place, and are attributed rather to the violence of storms, than to the ignorance of commanders. Some shipmasters never meet with accidents at sea, while others are a continued drain upon underwriters, by carrying away spars and sails. But that instinctive prudence which warns a man when to shorten sail, is a rare virtue on land as well as at sea.

I soon discovered that our officers, though old sailors, were entirely deficient of judgment; and they seemed as thoughtless as children about making and taking in sail, and I began to feel apprehensive of danger. The weather was so changeable that we were rarely allowed to sleep out our entire four hours below, being turned out continually, either to make or shorten sail. Hardly would we get warm in our berths, when there would come a thumping upon deck above our heads, and the gruff voice of one of the watch would roar out, "Larboard watch a-h-o-o-o-y! tumble up, tumble up, and shorten sail." This at last became so unpleasant, that the chief mate, in whose watch I was stationed, seeing a squall to leeward one dark night, swore he would reef topsails without turning up the other watch, hoping that they would be induced to imitate the example. This we could have done without difficulty, if he had made the attempt in season; but he delayed it, with his usual foolhardiness, until the squall struck us, and then tried to carry out his designs, for he was one of those foolishly resolute men, who will persist in an attempt when they see that success is impossible. In order to increase his force, he called the man on the lookout away from his post, and placed a boy at the wheel; and when we had succeeded in hauling out the reef-tackles of the mizzen topsail, he sent everybody aloft, thus leaving the ship, in the commencement of a threatening

4*

squall, with nobody on deck but himself to take care of her. The sailors murmured as they went aloft at the danger we were unnecessarily incurring, and vented a torrent of abusive oaths upon the head of the foolish mate. He was an old sea-dog, who had been several times wrecked, and received complimentary silver watches from passengers, and a gold chronometer from the board of underwriters, for his fearlessness and faithful conduct in times of peril, and for getting ships out of danger in which his own folly had placed them. He seemed never easy unless the wind was blowing a hurricane, and the straining masts were threatening to go by the board.

We had but just gained the topsail-yard, and were beginning to haul out the earings, when we heard a terrible crash, a loud scream, and at the same time we were almost thrown from the yard, by a shock as if the ship had struck upon the bottom. We could not see what had happened, but thought that the foremast had been carried away by the squall. It was very dark, but I saw a streak of foam in the water like that made by the track of a ship, which I supposed was occasioned by a whirlwind. We hurried upon deck, and there found that we had been run into by a ship sailing before the wind with all the canvass she could stagger under. The captain and passengers had jumped upon deck in their night clothes, and the greatest consternation prevailed for a short time, until it was found that we were not in a sinking state. The wind blew so strong that the ship which struck us soon drifted out of sight; and from her disappearing so suddenly, we thought she had gone down, and that all on board had perished. But we afterwards learned that she sustained but a trifling injury. Our own damage was very serious; the ship had struck us on the cut-water, and swept everything off, bowsprit, head, sails and all. There was a tremendous sea running at the time, and had we been struck a foot more inboard, the ship must have sunk before it would have been possible to clear away our boats. The accident, which seemed unavoidable, was the effect of pure carelessness and imprudence. If the man at the lookout had not been called away from his post, the ship would have been seen in time to have been avoided.

We lay to until daylight, hard at work, clearing away the wreck, and then squared our yards, and put back for the Cove of Cork, where we arrived on New-year's morning.

# CHAPTER IV.

## THE COVE.

HERE we were compelled to discharge our cargo into lighters; and as our captain and passengers were impatient of delay, we had to work until midnight by lanterns, in getting the ship in order for sea. We had a sore time of it, for it rained nearly every day, and our work was too urgent to allow us any rest, except on Sunday, and then but little. But this little was the sweeter for its rarity; and I enjoyed one Sunday afternoon ashore at the Cove, and thought more of the privilege, than I had of all the time I had spent in travelling at my ease over England and Scotland.

I had discovered in Liverpool, that virtue and content might dwell together in a cellar and be happy, with a meat dinner once a week,—a truth that I had no conception of before; and here I found that beauty and innocence could grow up in a garret, and thrive upon potatoes and buttermilk. Although there were several men-of-war in the harbour, a New-York liner being a very rare bird in these waters, and the most extravagant stories having been told of the magnificence of our ship's interior arrangements, caused our crew to be regarded in a more favourable light than any of the sailors belonging to the other ships. We were the elect of the best society, and received many attentions from the washer-women and small whiskey dealers, which made us the envy of the other crews on liberty. One of our crew, who was, in fact, a native of Cork, introduced us to his relations,—among the rest, a highly respectable widow, who traded in snuff and small marine stores. He had boasted a good deal of his aunt and her store, and he took me there alone, as if it would not comport with his aunt's pretensions, to bring the whole crew of common sailors to her house. We found this excellent lady sitting at the entrance of her warehouse, selecting out bits of nails and rusty screws from a heap of scrappy old iron; she was delighted to see her nephew, Dennis, and invited us to walk into the parlour and be comfortable. It was just in the dusk of the evening, so that the parlour was not very light, and being illuminated only by such particles of the sun's beams as could make their way through a little window of oiled paper, it was not easy at a glance to discover all that it contained; not that it was a very magnificent apartment as to its dimensions, or very much crowded with curious furniture; on the contrary, the floor was clay, very hard though, and tidily swept, and the walls were close together. I heard a singular noise in one corner of the parlour, and perceiving that the widow seemed anxious to hide the cause of it, I was not over curious to try to discover it; but the mystery soon cleared itself up; a full grown pig started up from a bundle of straw, and ran squealing past me into the street. The widow apologized for his rudeness, and said that he was not in the habit of coming into the house, but that his companion had been killed the day before, and he was lonesome, and had come into the parlour for companionship. Could a better reason have been given for a pig being found in one's parlour? I have seen guests in parlours since, whose presence could not be accounted for in half so satisfactory a manner. After tasting a drop of the widow's poteen, and leaving with her a small package of black tea, we repaired to the house of Mrs. Donovan, another widow lady; for I found that

nearly the entire female population of the Cove consisted of widows, who lived in a superior manner in
the attic of a tall house, whose chimneys were only
even with the terrace of the hill on the side of which
it was built. Mrs. Donovan was a *blanchisseuse;*
I dare not speak plainer, and must trust to the
reader being within reach of a French and English
dictionary ; and if there is anything in her professional calling calculated to impart such a sweetness
of temper, such a very tempting complexion, such
dazzling teeth, and so soft a voice as she possessed,
I should recommend all the ladies of my acquaintance to adopt it in preference, not only to any other,
but in preference to doing nothing. It is true, her
hands were not so white and corpse-like as the
hands of idler ladies are used to be, but they were
more plump and soft for the exercise of her calling.
But what was the widow Donovan, by the side of
her daughter Bridget! A coal droger by the side
the Queen's yacht; a goose by the side of a turtle
dove; a hollyhock by a moss rose. She was the
widow Donovan, in short, by the side of her daughter Bridget. Bridget Donovan had budded and
blossomed in the very garret in which I saw her,
probably ignorant of the luxury of a stocking during
the greater part of her life; she was only sixteen,
and as beautiful and bewitching as innocence, youth
and beauty could render her. Although she spoke
English well enough, she could prattle her native
Greek, and sing it too, like a bird; she had a voice
like a bob-o-link, and seemed as happy. We did
not visit without an invitation. No, indeed. Her
mother gave a *soiree,* expressly in our honour. All
the liners were there, some wearing white shirts
and frock coats, with breast-pins and satin stocks.
O, it was a beautiful time ! There were many
other ladies beside the widow and her daughter,
and many beautiful ones, too, but they were nothing

by the side of Bridget. I wondered at their venturing where their charms must be compared with hers; but it was fortunate they came: else there would have been fighting, and perhaps bloodshed, in striving for the honour of sitting by the widow's daughter.

When we first came in we had poteen, (it was before Father Mathew's day,) and afterwards wheaten cakes, with butter and coffee; unusual luxuries, I fear, in the sky-parlour of the widow Donovan! Then we had songs, genuine Irish melodies, not such faint things as you hear in theatres and concert rooms, nor such words as you find in Tom Moore, but better, a good deal better. More poteen and dancing. Reels, three-handed, five-handed, and seven-handed. And I danced with Bridget Donovan, set after set, and I felt very happy. I knew that I ought not to be,—that I had more cause for grief than merriment,—that I was out of my proper sphere, in a low situation, herding with people in whose company I should not be seen; but I could not help it: I never enjoyed myself better; and when it was time to go, I began to dream how delightful it would be to stay altogether. I bade farewell to Bridget, and have never seen her again, excepting in my dreams.

Dennis, who had introduced us to his aunt, gave me another instance of his partiality. While we were reloading one day he called me aside, and told me he had formed a high opinion of my abilities, and knew I was a lad he could depend upon, and asked me if I had a mind to join him in a little speculation. I asked for an explanation. He said the mate trusted to him every night to lock up the hatches, and as we are now taking on board bales of cloth, he had selected one which he judged, from its size and weight, must be fine broadcloth, and had hid it between decks, with an intention of leaving the forward hatch unlocked, and during his watch on deck taking it up and stowing it away in his berth. But as he couldn't well do it alone, he offered to give me half the spoils if I would assist him. I knew if I refused that he would persuade another of his shipmates to join him, and if they were detected they would suspect me of informing against them. So I listened to his proposition, and without assenting to it, told him to let me know when he was ready. He pointed the bale out to me during the day, which he had rolled aside, and I contrived, just before the hatches were closed, to jump down between decks and tumbled it into the lower hold without being perceived. He went to look after it that night, and was in a great rage when he found that it had been removed. The next day he selected another, which I disposed of in the same manner, and after that I contrived to give a hint to the second mate that he had better see the hatches secured himself. Dennis never suspected that I was not as great a rogue as himself, for he was very friendly during the passage, and rendered me many little kindnesses, which I did not hesitate to accept, for I considered he was indebted to me for saving him from committing a theft. But sailors have a very loose morality in regard to a ship's cargo, which is not owing so much to their want of honesty as to an instinctive feeling that they are themselves parts of the vessel, and have a right to anything on board of her, which the tyranny of their commander hinders them from enjoying. But in the case of Dennis I fear that there was something more than this feeling, and that he really had an unlawful hankering after other people's goods, for he had the misfortune, not long afterwards, to get confined in the tombs for something or other, I never knew exactly what.

There is a large Roman Catholic church in the Cove of Cork, which speaks more for the zeal than the taste or wealth of its builders. The poor people regard it with a good deal of religious pride, and I heard some very marvellous stories about its erection. A man with some pretensions to intelligence told me, that a few years ago there was an English Admiral on the station who had a residence on shore, in the rear of the church, and finding that it shut out his view of the harbour, he threatened to pull it down. The priest, hearing of his threat, called upon the Admiral, and found him sitting in an arm chair in his library.

" I have been told," said the priest, " that you have threatened to pull down our chapel, because it interrupts your prospect."

" I have," replied the Admiral gruffly, " have you anything to say against it ?"

" I have this to say," replied the priest, making a mysterious sign with his finger ; " sit you in that chair until you promise to leave our chapel untouched by your sacrilegious hand."

The priest looked sternly upon him, and the Admiral attempted to rise, but could not move a finger. He found himself fastened to his chair by some unseen power, and he begged the priest to release him ; but the priest would not, until he had made a vow not only to let the chapel alone, but never to commit any act of violence against any of the children of the holy Catholic church.

My informant had entire faith in this marvellous story, and I did not offend him by seeming to doubt it ; but I was relating the circumstance to a learned friend, a short time since, who, instead of laughing with me at the simplicity of the credulous Catholic, reproved my own want of faith, and said he believed the story himself, and began gravely to explain to me that the priest was undoubtedly a mesmerizer, who, instead of making a mysterious sign with his finger, had mesmerized the Admiral by a few passes of his hand. But I doubt whether the Catnolic himself would be willing to believe the story on such scientific terms.

We remained in the Cove of Cork three weeks, and put to sea again in good order; we cleared the land with a fair breeze, and I was beginning to anticipate a short passage, when the want of prudence and good judgment, that had led to our first disaster, very soon produced another almost as serious.

# CHAPTER V.

### THE PASSAGE.

Our captain was a rash, petulant man, witho t any of the generous roughness of a sailor, but with all his domineering and unfeeling vices. He prided himself on his gentlemanly qualities, having been well educated, and being the son of a rich merchant; he had no sympathy with his crew, and neither appreciated their efforts in times of difficulty, nor understood or cared to alleviate their hardships. Before leaving Cork some of the men applied to him for money to furnish themselves with shoes and other articles of dress, which our stay there had rendered necessary. One man in particular, who was very destitute, and had only one pair of thin shoes to last him the passage home, asked for money enough to pay for a pair of boots; but he refused to advance a shilling for any of them. Although he should have known that suitable clothing was as necessary for his crew to enable them to do their duty, as sails and rigging were for his ship. But he not only refused to advance any money to his crew, or provide them with proper clothing, but he neglected to lay in any extra provisions, although the ship had only enough on board for an ordinary passage when she left New-York. But he neglected nothing for his own comfort or that of his passengers, laying in a fresh stock of provisions, sheep, poultry, hampers of ale and soda water, and every imaginable delicacy which the port would produce. And he was right in doing so: but he was as regardless of his own interests as of the welfare of the

men under his command, in neglecting to furnish
food enough to last the passage.

Although we left the channel with a fair breeze,
in a day or two it changed to the southwest, and we
had repeated squalls, which threatened to blow our
masts away. One night the wind lulled a little, but
the sky still looked threatening, and though the
wind was dead in our teeth, the mate began to make
sail,—shaking the reefs out of the topsails, and set-
ting the main top-gallant sail. The men grumbled
at his folly, for they knew it would not be long before all hands must be called to shorten sail again.
We had hardly set the top-gallant sail, when the
wind began to pipe louder and louder; but as the
mate had but just made sail, he was ashamed to
take it in again before the ropes were coiled up. The
men saw that a squall was coming, and stationed
themselves, without being ordered, at the halliards,
ready to let them run at a moment's warning. The
wind increased so rapidly that the mate was obliged
to cry out, "call all hands to shorten sail;" but before the order could be executed, whew came the
blast out of a pile of mountainous-looking black
clouds, and the ship was on her beam ends. Crash,
crash, went the jib-boom and maintop-gallant mast;
the topsail halliards were all let go by the run; the
main tack parted, and the ship righted, but the wind
continued as fierce as ever; and what with its roaring and screeching, the hissing of the sea, the bang-
ing of the broken spars, the flapping of sails, and
thrashing of ropes, such a wild hubbub prevailed,
that it was impossible to hear the orders of the captain, and we all worked at sixes and sevens on our
own responsibility. Here was another night and
another day spent in clearing away the wreck; no
rest, no refreshment, save dry salt beef and hard
bread; and at work we went again, getting out a
new jib-boom and a new maintop-gallant mast. Be-

fóre they were rigged, the wind came out fair, a light easterly breeze, which for want of sails did us but little good. It was ten days before we got the ship in order again, and then we had another change of wind, and more squalls from the northwest. Three of our men gave out from sheer exhaustion, and were compelled to remain below, one of them mainly for the want of clothes, which the captain had refused to furnish him.

The day after our jib-boom was rigged we had another blow, and all hands were called again to shorten sail. The wind was from northwest, accompanied with hail squalls; the hail stones were as hard as pebbles; our hands and faces were sorely bruised with them, and it was with great difficulty that we could cling to the yards in reefing and furling. We were nearly four hours in getting things snug aloft; and just as the watch was going below, the captain thought it advisable to furl the mainsail, and all hands were again turned up. When we got upon the main yard the sail was stiff with hail and ice, and not being well hauled up, it was impossible to furl it. We tried the best we could do, but we could do nothing: ten minutes spent on deck in hauling the sail up, would have enabled us to furl in as short a time. But the captain and mate stood upon the quarter deck, sipping hot coffee; and feeling warm and comfortable, they amused themselves by calling us a pack of old soldiers, and threatening to keep us there until morning if we did not furl the sail. It was to no purpose that we called out to them to haul up the bunt-lines and leech-lines; they only replied to us by damning our eyes, and calling us Mahon soldiers. We had now been more than six hours aloft, and were nearly exhausted; whether we should have made out to cling much longer to the yard is doubtful. The captain went below, and the mate then ordered us down, and told us to haul the sail up snug, which we did, and went aloft again to furl it. The wind had increased to a hurricane, and the waves ran higher than I had ever seen them before. The sun had gone down, but the sky was clear, and the foam of the sea made it as light as noon. We were not long in furling the sail; but while we were on the yard a long rolling sea, a huge mountain of brine, broke upon deck and buried the ship completely under water; it reared its foaming crest so high as to wet us on the yard. Fortunately nobody was washed overboard; but the sea carried away the cook's galley, filled the cabin full of water, and washed away the forecastle scuttle, so that they were forced to nail boards on its entrance to keep the ship from being swamped; and when we came down upon deck, frozen, weary and hungry, we had no place to retreat to—for such an enormity as taking a sailor into the cabin of a liner, in the presence of passengers, was never heard of or dreamed of. The mate, seeing that we were like to die, very compassionately gave each of us a gill of raw whiskey, which I drank without winking; but I was chilled so thoroughly that I never felt it after it got down my throat. At another time it would have taken me off my feet.

I am entirely in favour of temperance, even total abstinence; but if I were a captain or owner of a ship, she should never go to sea without whiskey. Hot coffee, and hot ginger and water, are unquestionably excellent substitutes for ardent spirits; but there are occasions at sea when hot water cannot be had; and some kind of stimulant is necessary, if not to preserve life, at least to impart enough to enable men to preserve the ship.

We remained on deck until midnight, when the watch, whose turn it was to go below, went down the fore hatch, and creeping over the coal and salt between decks, made out to knock off some boards from the forecastle bulkhead, and get into the forecastle, which we found knee deep in water. All our beds and clothes were soaking wet; and instead of sleeping, we had to go to work and bale up the water, and hang up our clothing to dry.

It was now nearly a month since we left Cork, and we had not made a third of our distance; the wind was ahead, the weather was cold, and my clothes were beginning to give out. I had enjoyed capital health, had an appetite like a horse, and slept soundly whenever I got a chance. Constant practice had made me perfectly familiar with my duty, and I could run about the rigging with any man on board. Notwithstanding all our buffetings, we had our songs and stories, and some very good singers and romancers we had too. We now found that our provisions were getting short, and we were put upon a very meagre allowance of bread and beef, although we were allowed a plenty of potatoes and salt. But potatoes were watery food for stomachs that had to endure the cold and toil of our ship's deck; and many a night when I turned into my bunk I was too hungry to sleep. Another fortnight passed without any marked disaster, when we encountered a gale from the southwest, compared with which all other tornadoes were mere zephyrs. Like all southwesters, it gave timely notice of its approach; and had our officers been possessed of seaman-like prudence, half its disastrous consequences might have been avoided. We shortened sail in good season, leaving nothing set but a close-reefed fore and main topsail, mizzen staysail, and fore-topmast staysail; but we neglected to put preventer braces upon the fore and main yards, in consequence of which the strain of the topsails sprung the main yard, and carried away the fore yard in the slings; we lost our new jib-boom, all three topsails and main top-gallant sail. They had all been snugly furled, but they were blown into shreds and ribbons. For seven or eight hours we were at the mercy of the gale, unable to do more than secure ourselves to the deck. It was a frightful sight to see·our ship, with her broken spars held by their chain fastenings, and blown out upon the wind like feathers, the ropes and sails fluttering, snapping and cracking, flying before it, now buried between cavernous waves, and now thrust up into the upper world, as though she were in the power of some malicious demon who was wreaking his vengeance upon her in the wantonness of malice. For the first time our captain seemed to forget his formal consequence, and while clinging to the ring-bolts to save his life, appeared to feel that he was in the keeping of a power greater than himself. If he had any such thoughts, they subsided with the storm, for as soon as we were able to go to work upon the wreck, he was as petulant, as trifling, and as ill-natured as ever. We had now to get up a new fore yard, a new jib-boom, to fish the main yard, and bend an entire new suit of sails, and try to make something out of the remnants of the old ones that were left. Here was unmitigated hard work all night and all day ; three or four of our sailors were on the sick list, and our allowance of beef and bread had grown so scant, that even with all the help of potatoes and salt, we suffered from hunger. The mates had their hot coffee every morning brought to them as soon as the cook got a fire under his coppers, and our chattering teeth were only set on edge by seeing them sip it. While we were working upon the main yard, I chanced to cast my eyes down the sky-light into the cabin, and saw the captain and his passengers at their breakfast. A sheep had been slaughtered the day before, and they had mutton chops, fried ham, hot rolls, buckwheat cakes, omelets, tea and coffee, and boiled milk. I had been on deck nearly the whole night, my clothes were wet, and I had just come from my own breakfast, which consisted of nothing more than a kid of boiled potatoes; for while I was carrying my pot of tea from the cook's galley to the forecastle, a little jet of spray had leaped over the bow and fallen plump into it and spoiled it. I could get no more. I was very hungry, and for the first time I thought of my former comforts; the cabin breakfast had such a natural look, and seemed to belong to me as a matter of right.

The inequalities of civilized life, where one portion of the people are privileged to live without work, and the other portion are doomed to work without living, are more perceptible on ship-board than in any other condition of life. Here are twenty or thirty men, afloat upon the ocean, confined to a space so small that they cannot get out of each other's hearing, yet dwelling apart from each other as though they belonged to different worlds, and had no wants in common. At one end of the vessel which contains them live ten men, who are carefully screened from the cold and wet; their hands are soft, their sleep undisturbed, and every good thing which the earth, air or ocean produces is procured for their appetites; they are the superfine of the earth,—gods that have neither cares nor duties,—birds in gilt cages, that are not required even to sing in return for the lumps of white sugar that are thrust between the wires. At the other end of the vessel are ten other men, upon whose exertions the lives and fortunes of the other ten depend; these are exposed to every danger; they brave the lightning, their faces are pelted by hail, they are soaked in spray, they toil unceasingly, their food is coarse and scant, their hours of rest uncertain; no kind words are spoken to them; their wishes are

never consulted, and they are beaten if they think
or dare to act contrary to the will of those whose
lives depend upon their exertions. Idlers should
be content to be idlers ; they should at least allow
those who labour to enjoy an equal portion of the
fruits of their own industry.

Our bread and meat were reserved for dinner ;
there was but little of either, and one man was ap-
pointed to divide it into eleven equal parts, the
number of our watch ; he was a natural mathemati-
cian, and succeeded in dividing the little bits of
gristle and crumbs of bread into hexagon heaps, as
exactly of a size as the cells in a bee hive. But to
prevent anything like favouritism, after he had made
the division, we blindfolded him, and one of us pointed
to a heap and said, " Who shall have this ?" " Donovan." " Who shall have this ?" " Futtuck ;" and
so on until the whole was disposed of. All this,
though disheartening enough, was made a subject of
merriment, and we had our songs through it all, and
laughed at our miseries. And such stories as we
had ! a perfect library of romance. Every man in
the watch was a character, and had passed through
as many strange adventures as Sinbad. They were
all good fellows, without a particle of meanness in
them, and they never hung back to avoid danger, or
work, or wet. But one of our number was consti-
tutionally heavy ; not lazy, but sanguineous ; fat and
good-tempered. He wouldn't work if he could avoid
it, and liked sleeping better than anything in the
world. He must have had pleasant dreams, and no
doubt preferred them to the hard-featured realities
of his waking hours. He was not indifferent to eating, but sleep was his pet enjoyment. Once he fell
sound asleep on the topsail yard, with a shower of
hail beating in his face. What could have tempted
such a man to go to sea I could not learn. His
name was George, a fat, heavy name ; he had a

broad, good-humoured, ruddy countenance, and the richest voice for a sentimental song that ever piped in a forecastle. Nobody disliked him, because he was always in a good humour, and it was not easy to think of famine with such a fat subject before you. Sailors have sometimes been put to strange straits, and have liked a shipmate the better for being fat. The world is full of antagonists, and George had his in our forecastle—a sharp, bustling, discontented, sleepless, planning, ill-natured, hungry blue-nose from Nova Scotia. He had once been chief mate of a two-topsail schooner, and could never forget his present degradation, as he seemed to consider it, long enough to take anything easy. He was always hunting after his knife or his tin pot, and never failed to quarrel with the cook whenever he went to the galley for his pot of tea. At his meals he was sure to remember some Nova Scotia delicacy, such as a leg of smoked mutton, or a dried halibut's fin, that he would have had for his dinner if he had been at home.

It is very strange that men who have once been up in the world, should think it necessary to make themselves wretched, by continually dwelling upon their former grandeur, when they happen to fall to a lower sphere; and yet it is natural enough. The devils in hell would not be half so wretched if they had not once been inhabitants of heaven. But this is not a just analogy. The fall from innocence to guilt can only produce unmitigated bitterness; but such a fall as our Nova Scotian's, from smoked mutton to salt and potatoes, ought not to rumple the pin-feathers of an independent mortal. Another man might have grumbled over a dried halibut's fin, although such a delicacy would have filled up the measure of our grumbler's content. The best way is to grumble at nothing, and make the best of what

we can get, even though it may not be the fill of our
desires.

The remainder of our crew were very good
sailors, and were always ready to perform their
duty, when they were not prevented by illness, else
we should have had a more terrible time of it.
Every nation in Europe was represented in our
forecastle : there were two Swedes, one Dane, one
Norwegian, three Scotch, one Irish, one Prussian,
one Pole, one Frenchman, one Welshman, one
Hanoverian, six English, one American, myself, and
two English boys.  Not a soul of them had been
naturalized, even; and yet our laws say that none
but American citizens shall serve as sailors on board
of our ships.   But such laws are made to be broken.
How absurd it would be to pass a law to prevent
any but American citizens serving as waiters in our
hotels, or to hinder foreigners from carrying the
hod, or digging our canals.   But such a law would
not be a jot more absurd than that which is meant
to keep foreigners out of our ships.   Indeed it would
not be half so absurd ; for we have one law that says
that none but American citizens shall serve on board
our ships, and another that virtually excludes them
from such employment.   We have hardly a statute
in our books that is not contradicted by another, but
none so absurdly as the laws for creating the mate-
rials for a navy.   The one ruling motive with Americans in adopting a profession, is the hope of preferment, and where that is denied to them, they
cannot be enticed to enter.   Our laws, therefore, by
denying preferment to the seamen of our navy, let
their merits be what they may, deprive Americans
of every honourable inducement to serve their country as sailors, and even make the badge of the navy
a disgrace to those who wear it.   For nothing can
be more disgraceful to an honest American, than to
accept of a situation where promotion is denied to

him. The poorest boy in the nation may aspire to
the highest office in the gift of his countrymen; but
if he should enter the navy as a sailor, though he had
the spirit of a Decatur, he could never rise a single
step beyond the degraded condition of a serving
man. The effect of a regulation like this could be
easily foreseen, and it was foreseen by the time-
serving place-hunters who framed it, who knew that
no American, unless he were degraded by vice,
would ever enter a national ship, and therefore to
compel Americans to do so, they framed a law, de-
claring that none but American citizens should
navigate either our national or merchant vessels.
And were any attempt made to enforce this law, our
ships would rot at our wharves and navy-yards.
There should be no more disgrace in serving as a
sailor on board our war ships, than in serving as a
clerk in the War Department at Washington; and
there would not be, if the line of promotion in our
naval service were thrown open to the deserving.
In what manner, or by whose ill-judgment the
ridiculously aristocratic regulations of our naval
service were imposed upon the nation, I know not;
but a more efficient plan for destroying that arm of
our national defence, could not have been devised
by our bitterest enemy. The navy of no nation in
the world is so hampered and enervated by such
exclusive and aristocratic regulations as ours.

It may be asked, in what manner are the laws
regarding sailors evaded? Nothing is more easy.
Two thirds of the sailors in our ships perjure themselves; and so lightly are such false oaths regarded,
that they are among sailors a common subject for
mirth; and certificates of citizenship are bartered
for knives or plugs of tobacco.

There is but one way in which American seamen
can be made, and that is by throwing open the line
of promotion in the navy. As long as the officers

in the service are selected from the sons of political favourites, without regard to their fitness, our national and merchant vessels will continue to be manned by the drippings of European navies ; and if war should ever again call for a naval force, we should have to begin at the beginning, and create sailors, the same as though we had not spent hundreds of millions to maintain a navy in time of profound peace.

## CHAPTER VI.

WHILE we were engaged in repairing the damages of the last gale, we were tantalized by another haul of easterly wind, which died away before we got in a condition to use it. We had kept well to the northward, anticipating a prevalence of northerly winds; but our hardest gales had been from the southwest, which had driven us into such a high latitude that the cold was very severe, and our decks were all the time covered with hail. Our ship was a fast sailer and a good sea-boat; but being deeply laden with a dead cargo, she laboured heavily, and when there was much wind, the sea made a continual breach across her bows, so that when we had, by any lucky chance, kept our clothes dry for a whole watch, we usually got well soaked in attempting to go below. Yet, notwithstanding that we were literally under water more than half our time, we were compelled to wash the ship's deck every morning at daybreak, without any regard to the weather, if we could stand on our feet long enough to carry a bucket of water to the mate, who would dash it upon the deck with a perfectly grave face, although at the time the sea would be making a breach over us. But it is the universal custom at sea to wash down a ship's decks at daylight, whether it be necessary or not.

We had laboured under a great disadvantage in making our last repairs, from having lost our carpenter a few days before the last gale. As the cause of his death was peculiar, it will require some remarks before I relate it.

A ship's deck is an absolute monarchy, where the

chief officer holds unchecked sway over the lives
and pleasures of his people.   There are no constitu-
tional balances at sea.   The captain can do no wrong.
The laws of the deck are made for the protection
of the king, who, having absolute command, needs
no protection ; his orders must be obeyed without
thought ; to question them is mutiny ; his humours
must be regarded as divine wisdom ; his tyranny is
only discipline.   Right or wrong, his word is a law
that cannot be broken with impunity.   If from
weakness or meekness he allows the transgressor
to escape, the law seizes him and punishes him
ashore.   If a sailor raise his hand in self-defence
against his superior in command, 'tis mutiny ; if he
is starved, he is not allowed the privilege of complaint ; if he is overworked, he can claim no extra
pay ; if he refuse to work, his pay is stopped.   He
may be ordered aloft at the peril of his life, ay,
where death would be certain, to save a bit of rope
not worth a shilling; and if he refuse to go, he can
be put in irons and tried for a capital offence.   The
authority of a ship-master, like that of a slave-owner,
is too great not to be abused.   It is not in human
nature to resist the temptation to tyranny that our
law holds out to ship-masters.   Men cannot help
holding in contempt those over whom they exercise
unlimited control.   The prerogatives of tyranny
smother all kindly feelings in the human breast, and
therefore they should in all cases be forbidden by law,
and not established as they are in the case of a sea-
commander.   There is nothing in the relation of a
ship-captain to his crew, which requires such a wide
distinction as the law makes between them.   A sailor has the same instinctive feelings of self-preservation which other men have, which would lead him
to obey his commander in times of difficulty, and
which should allow him the privilege of expostula-
tion, when he sees his superior is unfit to command.

There is no better reason for giving the master of a ship unlimited power over his crew, than there is for giving the same authority to a mechanic over his apprentices or journeymen.

The great error of our naval discipline is its being adopted from the British service, in which it is perfectly consistent with the other departments of the government; with us it is a monstrous anomaly, a foul blot upon our free system of laws. In truth, our marine is governed by a code greatly inferior to that of England; for while she has made many improvements, we have stood still. Merit may do something towards promoting a man in any European naval service; but in ours, the most worthless poltroon, whose friends possess political influence sufficient to gain him an appointment in our navy, rises side by side to pay and station, with the brightest and best spirits in the service. No government in Europe is half so exclusive, so tyrannical, so aristocratic in regard to its subjects who act as its defenders, as ours to its citizens. A Nelson, a Decatur, might serve in our navy until he was gray, and never be rewarded with promotion.

The strange darkness of the public mind in regard to this matter has recently been sadly developed in the case of the horrible murders committed on board the Somers. View that terrible transaction as you may, with all the apologies of the main actor in the unparalleled tragedy before you, and it must be accounted a cowardly murder. I am exceedingly unwilling to allude to a subject which must be alike painful to the friends of the unhappy victims of our tyrannical laws, and to those of the ill-judging officers who acted as their executioners. But the subject is one of too great importance to allow it to be passed by, when it will serve to illustrate the evils which the people can only remove by being made acquainted with them.

6*

We have been maintaining a naval force for nearly thirty years, at an expense to the industry of the nation exceeding two hundred millions of dollars; and all the glory that we have earned in return has been the capture of two feeble towns,* whose inhabitants had done us no wrong, and for which we were compelled to make apologies, and court-martial the captors; and the murder, in cool blood, of three unarmed men, who were hung at the yard-arm of a national ship, without even being tried, or informed of their offence. It is the foulest, darkest, bloodiest spot upon our national history. Although perpetrated by one or two individuals, it is a national offence, because it was the legitimate result of our national LAW; and because the deed itself has been approved by the public voice. It was the inevitable effect of a system, miscalled of defence, which has reared in the midst of our boasted democracy, an absurd aristocracy, at variance with our beautiful system, which, beyond all other human governments, helps to restore humanity to its rights. The wisdom of Washington is misinterpreted by us. In time of peace prepare for war, is a caution to avoid war by practising the arts of peace, and not to hasten it on by arming ships and fortifications, and thus creating a war-spirit in our bosoms when we have not an enemy in the world, and all the world is in profound peace. The true watch-word of the nation is, *in time of war prepare for peace.* No man thinks of going into the street with a sword in his hand, lest an enemy should attack him, when he knows of no enemy. Why then should a nation keep itself in a state of warlike defence, when no one attempts to make an aggression ?

The unequaled outrage committed on board the

---

* The capture of Foxardo by Com. Porter, and of Monterey by Captain Jones.

Somers, should have opened the eyes of our people to the enormous wrongs that they were nursing in their navy; but the leaven of aristocracy which was left in our laws at the time of our dissolution with England, has not yet worked out, and the fresh supplies which we continue to receive from her in our daily reading, must account for the unnatural verdict of the public mind in regard to this matter.

With a kind of bitter irony, but not less severe for that, the inhabitants of Boston or Philadelphia, I forget which city has a right to this honour, bestowed upon the cowardly actor in that dreadful tragedy, a sword. A Sword! What should he do with a sword? In judging of a case like the inhuman massacre on board the Somers, we might safely trust to the verdict of British officers, without any fear of leaning on the side of mercy. But the voice of the British navy, speaking through its acknowledged organs, pronounces the act one of the most dastardly and inhuman that has ever been perpetrated upon the ocean.

Men who live on shore, see a mist whenever they look out to sea. Every thing with them suffers a sea change. Mariners are a strange kind of monsters to them; with unnatural proportions and distorted passions; they live at sea, out of the pale of the sweet charities which encompass them on shore; they are laughed at and wondered at as odd fish, and are not sympathized with as men possessing human feelings, and subject to suffering from the wrongs which oppress other men.

The chief mate of our ship was a model quarter-deck tyrant; too much of a man to be despised, and too bad a one to be respected. He had all the elements of a tyrant in him; he was courageous, revengeful, and capricious; sufficiently kind to his favourites to make it desirable to gain his good will. Towards some of us in the forecastle he manifested a fondness almost parental, bringing us dry stockings, plugs of tobacco, and sly drinks of whiskey. Sometimes he would even take off his jacket and throw it to some of the men who looked cold; while he would refuse others a patch of canvass to mend a tattered sou'wester. Towards me he evinced a partiality which added nothing to my comfort, for it made me an object of suspicion with my companions in the forecastle, upon whom I was more dependent than upon the officers. The friendship of a tyrant is always dangerous. Sometimes he would call me aft, and under a pretence of keeping me at work, he would make me stand inside the hurricane house during a whole watch, to keep me out of the wet.

Our second mate was an amiable young man, ambitious of getting ahead, and a good sailor enough for one of his age. But the mate treated him worse than a dog, and I saw him sometimes shed tears when the mate "blew him up," as he called his abuse. Every mishap that occurred on board the ship was attributed to the unfortunate second mate, who was rarely called by any other name than a Mahon soldier. " Don't fall, dummy," the mate would call out to him when he was aloft, in a sneering voice. Every epithet of contempt that he could invent was bestowed by the mate upon the unfortunate second dickey, until the poor fellow was harassed within an inch of his life. And yet, to have spoken or acted in his own defence would have been mutiny. The mate would not strike any body, because he had suffered in the Marine Court for doing so. Flogging a sailor at sea on board a merchant vessel, is an expensive amusement; but any other cruelty or abuse may be practised with impunity.

Our carpenter was another of the mate's buts. He was a Norwegian, a huge titanesque creature, who might have personated the god Woden, or any other of the beer-drinking heroes of the Northern mythology. He towered up above our heads with his broad scowling face, like a being of a different race. He was an old man, past sixty-five, and all his life had been spent at sea. It is inconceivable that a man could have lived so long upon the earth, and should know so little about it. A green leaf was as great a novelty to him as it was to Noah's dove. The greater part of his life had been spent on board of a Swedish frigate, where he had acquired a habit of obedience rarely found in an Englishman or an American. His shoulders were of immense breadth, but not an inch too broad for his ponderous head, which was but scantily provided with hair, that looked like steel wires. His face was brown, like a piece of old mahogany; and a scar on his right cheek, and another that divided his under lip on the left side, gave it a singular appearance of ferocity. His nose was enormous, full of holes, and in colour resembling a bunch of Isabella grapes, looking as if it had been used as a target by a rifle company; his eyes, which were a greenish blue, were shaded by a pair of heavy black eyebrows, as shaggy and hard looking as the dwarf cedars that frown upon the brow of a stony hill which I look upon from my window as I sit and write. These were very far from the elements of beauty, certainly; but grouped as they were on the person of old Derrick, they created an impression by no means unpleasant. He was mainly good-natured, but uncontrollable when excited to passion by an affront, and therefore we in the forecastle all took good care not to offend him: a blow from his fist was not a thing one would be likely to forget in a hurry. He would have been a most amusing companion, if it had been possible to understand him, for his wild northern stories were just the kind of amusement fitted to our stormy watches; but the scar in his lip, and his barbarous tongue together, made his at-

tempts at English the most incomprehensible jar-
gon that was ever uttered. He could understand
the orders given him, and he always executed them
faithfully, but we had to guess at his meaning when
ever he spoke. The mate took a fancy to torment
the carpenter, not from spite or malice, but from
the pure wantonness of tyranny: for no other reason
than that he had the power to do so. He used to
call Derrick leather-lips, instead of carpenter, which
vexed the soul of the old man the more because his
habit of duty would not allow him to make any reply, even though his imperfect speech would have
allowed him to do so.

"What now, leather-lips?" the mate would say,
when the carpenter stepped upon the quarter-deck;
at which the old man would knit his shaggy brows,
and stride back to the forecastle, venting his terrible northern curses, and gnashing his teeth horri-
bly. Sometimes he would be so vexed at the mate's
jokes, that he would not eat a mouthful for two or
three days. Instead of getting used to the mate's
banter, the old man grew more and more irritable,
and his paroxysms of passion became more frightful. He would sit upon his tool-chest, and mutter
something after this fashion: "Fut te tyvil in hell!
fut leffer-lips; I fill kill myself; I fill kill myself and
go to hell fit him. Fut te tyvil ist to leffer-lips. I
fill be tammed fit hell fit him."

Thus the old Norwegian giant would sit and
threaten; and the mate, so far from being moved
to pity by his unhappy petulance, would only laugh
at him, and say, "Go it while you're young, leather-
lips." He at last grew so petulant and wrathful
from the continued banter of the mate, that no one
in the forecastle dared to speak to him. One night
after a day of unusual fatigue, the old man came
down into the forecastle, and struck the lid of his
chest with his clenched fist, and swore a tremendous

oath, that the next time the mate called him by that hated name he would jump overboard and drown himself. His old eyes flashed fire as he spoke, and I was fearful that he would be as good as his word. During the night we had a very heavy blow from the southeast, but towards morning it died away, and by sunrise it was nearly calm, but as there was a little air, all hands were turned up to make sail; and while we were mast-heading the topsails, old Derrick came upon deck, and the mate called out, "Come aft here, leather-lips, and give us a pull."

The old man instantly pulled off his cap and jumped upon the railing forward of the main rigging, and standing erect, shook his fist at the mate.

"Get down, you old fool, or you will fall overboard," cried the mate. Derrick made no reply, but glared fiercely upon us, and leaped into the sea. The act was so sudden that we were all paralyzed for a moment, and the mate turned as pale as death, and trembled violently. We immediately threw overboard all the loose articles about deck, and in five minutes the stern boat was in the water. But the old man had disappeared for ever. It was nearly calm; and although there was a very heavy swell, we could have saved him, but it seemed that he had purposely held his head under water. The mate tried to make light of the matter, and said the old man was crazy; but it was very evident that he felt himself encumbered by the weight of a murdered fellow being.

The old man was a great annoyance to us the remainder of the voyage, for hardly a night passed that some of the crew did not fancy they either saw him or heard him; they always had called him a Fin, and they believed he had power to raise or allay the wind at his pleasure; and every unusual

gale we experienced the rest of the passage, tney
would say, " Old Derrick is giving it to us again."
Although it was known that he had a case bottle of
schnapps in his chest, not a soul had the courage to
touch it, fearing that he would appear to them if
they did.

## CHAPTER VII.

A CELEBRATED naval commander has said that mere courage is not sufficient for a sailor; he must be " fool-hardy;" but he must be more than this—an unconsciousness of hardship and peril will not do; he must love danger for its own sake, or he can be no genuine sailor. There are no inducements held out to sailors to make them in love with their fool-hardy business, but on the contrary, all the discouragements that would keep men from other employments. Owners and masters of ships understand perfectly well that sailors go to sea for pure enjoyment, and not for gain, and therefore they give them for their invaluable services the smallest pittance possible for them to subsist upon. A hod carrier is magnificently rewarded, compared with a sailor; a chambermaid, whose heaviest duty is in shaking up a bed, receives nearly the same wages as a foremast hand in our packet service. It is very clear that sailors do not go to sea for the sake of what they get, but from some other motive, which none but a sailor can comprehend. There may be some inquisitive spirits who go to sea for the sake of what they can see; but there are but few such. The genuine sailor is a reckless, daring spirit, whose hell is quiet. He must have strong and powerful excitements, such as only dallying with death produces. Generally he is as indifferent as the vessel he floats in about the length of his voyage or the port of its termination; the Gulf of Mexico and the Gulf of Finland are the same to him.

On board of our ship there was a sailor who never discovered, until we were out of the channel, that

7

we were bound to New-York instead of New-Orleans; he having shipped in a vessel bound to the
latter port. And when he discovered his mistake,
he said less about it than an omnibus traveller would
at being carried a block out of his way. One of our
crew told me of a strange incident in his life, occasioned by this carelessness of destination. He left
his native place in a brig bound to Havana, and after
his arrival in that port deserted his ship and went on
board of a slaver bound for the coast of Africa,
probably enticed by the peril of the employment,
and with the hope of being hung for a pirate. The
brig in which he had left home returned in due time,
and when in sight of port was wrecked, and every
soul on board perished. When the wreck was discovered, the friends of her crew took measures to
recover the bodies of their relations; and among the
rest, the father and brothers of the young sailor who
had been left behind, never having heard of his desertion, and supposing him drowned, as a matter of
course, were at great pains to recover his body. A
corpse was found upon the beach which they thought
was his; it was much defaced, but they had no doubt
of its identity, and therefore bestowed upon it due
funeral rites, and erected a marble stone over it in
the village burying ground, with an inscription
bearing as little truth, perhaps, as ever a tomb-stone
bore. The runaway was drifted about upon the
ocean two or three years, when, having been paid
off in Boston with money enough to buy a new suit
of clothes, he determined to go home and see his
mother. It was dusk when he reached his father's
door, and entering without ceremony, he found the
family seated at supper. The tumult and confusion
which followed his sudden appearance among them
must be left to the reader's imagination. The next
morning his father took him to the burying ground
and showed him the stone that had been erected to

his memory, and he enjoyed the pleasure, which has probably fallen to the lot of but few mortals, of reading his own epitaph; he told me there were some first rate lines on his tomb-stone, but he had forgotten them.

Sailors generally come from the country; the majority of them have worked on a farm. Town-bred youths are too effeminate for the sea; they have too many recollections of the delicacies and amusements of a city life to " scorn delights and live laborious days."

One of our crew was a young Englishman, who had the chivalrous disposition of a knight-errant; placed in a higher sphere, he would have been acknowledged the flower of gallantry. His name was Macartney; he told me that his brother was a major in the service of the East India Company, and that his aunt was the wife of an earl. His father was killed at the battle of Waterloo. But Jack required no extraneous honours; he was an honest fellow, and a brave-hearted gentleman—who might have lived ashore in ease, but he delighted in the dangers and hardships of a sea life. When our provisions were getting short, and it required the soul of a philosopher to resist the temptation of cutting a larger slice of beef than fell to your share, Jack would never help himself until every man in the watch had had his cut. On one occasion, when we had been kept from our dinner by some unnecessary work which the mate had put upon us for the sake of " working up" somebody whom he had taken a dislike to, on going down into the forecastle, we found the kids which contained our beef and pudding (duff, as the sailors call it,) capsized, and the contents rolling in the lee scuppers, cold and dirty. Everybody began to grumble at the bad treatment we received, and to complain of our cold dinner. But Jack sat looking on in silence, until he

saw one of the watch make a motion to cut a piece
of the beef..

"Avast there !" said Jack ; "are you going to
sit there, like dogs in a kennel, and growl and eat
whatever your master throws at you ? Take your
kids and go aft to the captain and tell him you will
not be fed like dogs." But nobody moved.

"Never mind ; I'll go myself," he said ; and
taking the kids in his hands he carried them on to
the quarter-deck, where the captain was walking
with his thumbs in the arm-holes of his vest.

"What do you want ?" said the captain, sternly.

"I want to be treated like a man, and not like a
brute," said Jack ; "see what has been served up
to us for our dinner; haven't we done our duty, and
more than our duty ?"

"Go forward, you mutinous rascal," said the captain, " or I will put you in irons."

"It will not be safe for you to attempt it," said
Jack. "But you are no gentleman, or you would
not talk to me in that manner."

The captain grew livid with rage, and called for
his pistols, which were immediately handed to him
by the steward.

"Poo ! poo !" said Jack, "you are a cowardly
wretch. I wont make a disturbance by taking hold
of you, but I'll thrash you as soon as we reach New-
York. We wont eat your dirty beef;" and so say-
ing, he threw the two kids overboard, and walked
forward.

"What ! have you thrown our grub overboard ?"
muttered one of the men.

"Yes," said Jack, " I have ; and if a soul of you
grumbles at it, I'll flog him."

So we ate dry bread for our dinner that day. It
was not long afterwards that the captain and his passengers lost their dinner, but didn't manifest much
heroism under their disappointment.

## CHAPTER VIII.

AMONG the luxuries which the captain had provided for himself and passengers was a fine green
turtle, which was not likely to suffer from exposure
to salt water, so it was reserved, until all the pigs,
and sheep, and poultry had been eaten. A few
days before we arrived, it was determined to kill
the turtle and have a feast the next day. Our cabin
gentlemen had been long enough deprived of fresh
meats to make them cast lickerish glances towards
their hard-skinned friend, and there was a great
smacking of lips the day before he was killed. As
I walked aft occasionally I heard them congratula-
ting themselves on their prospective turtle soup and
force-meat balls; and one of them, to heighten the
luxury of the feast, ate nothing but a dry biscuit for
twenty-four hours, that he might be able to devour
his full share of the unctuous compound. It was to
be a gala day with them; and though it was not
champagne day, that falling on Saturday and this on
Friday, they agreed to have champagne a day in
advance, that nothing should be wanting to give a
finish to their turtle. It happened to be a rougher
day than usual when the turtle was cooked, but they
had become too well used to the motion of the ship
to mind that. It chanced to be my turn at the wheel
the hour before dinner, and I had the tantalizing mi-
sery of hearing them laughing and talking about their
turtle, while I was hungry from want of dry bread
and salt meat. I had resolutely kept my thoughts
from the cabin during all the passage but once, and
now I found my ideas clustering round a tureen of
imaginary turtle in spite of all my philosophy. Con-

7*

found them, if they had gone out of my hearing with
their exulting smacks, I would not have envied their
soup; but their hungry glee so excited my imagination, that I could see nothing through the glazing of
the binnacle but a white plate with a slice of lemon on
the rim, a loaf of delicate bread, a silver spoon, a napkin, two or three wine glasses of different hues and
shapes, and a stream of black, thick, and fragrant
soup pouring into the plate.   By and by it was four
bells; they dined at six.   And all the gentlemen,
with the captain at their head, darted below into
the cabin, where their mirth increased when they
caught sight of the soup plates.  "Hurry with the
soup, steward," roared the captain.  "Coming, sir,"
replied the steward.   The cook opened the door of
his galley, and out came the delicious steam of the
turtle, such as people often inhale, and step across
the street of a hot afternoon to avoid, as they pass
by Delmonico's in South William-street.   Then came
the steward with a large covered tureen in his hand,
toward the cabin gangway.   I forgot the ship for a
moment in looking at this precious cargo, the wheel
slipped from my hands, the ship broached to with a
sudden jerk; the steward had got only one foot upon
the stairs, when this unexpected motion threw him off
his balance, and down he went by the run; the tureen
slipped from his hands, and part of its contents flew
into the lee scuppers, and the balance followed him
in his fall.

I laughed outright.   I enjoyed the turtle a thou-
sand times more than I should have done if I had
eaten the whole of it.   But I was forced to restrain
my mirth, for the next moment the steward ran upon
deck, followed by the captain in a furious rage, threatening if he caught him to throw him overboard.   Not
a spoonful of the soup had been left in the coppers,
for the steward had taken it all away at once to keep
it warm.   In about an hour afterwards the passen

gers came upon deck, looking more sober than I had seen them since we left Liverpool. They had dined upon cold ham.

On the first of March we got soundings on St. George's bank. Cold as it was before, the weather now grew colder. Hail was changed to snow, and our ship's decks were covered with ice; all the tacks and sheets were frozen stiff, and we were forced to keep away to the south to thaw out, for if we had been struck by a squall it would have been impossible to shorten sail. Before we could square our yards we had to pour hot water upon the tacks, to render them pliable enough to start them. It was so extremely difficult to work the ship, in consequence of the ice upon the running rigging, and the wind was so fresh, for we were under close-reefed topsails, that it was considered prudent to clue up the foresail while we were wearing ship, lest it should blow away; and it being discovered that one of the clue-garnets was stranded, I was sent aloft to secure it. I was chilled to the midriff before leaving the deck, and I had not been aloft many minutes before I began to feel benumbed and drowsy, and perceiving that I had lost the power of sustaining myself, I grasped my arms around the forward swifter, (one of the shrouds of the foremast,) and contrived to drop upon deck without injuring myself. How I did it I do not know, and at the time I did not care, for I was past feeling, and I remember that I had half a mind to drop myself overboard. I lost all consciousness as soon as I struck the deck, and being taken below, they poured some hot brandy and water down my throat, and in an hour or two I revived and went to my duty on deck. This was the only time during the passage that I was off duty an hour.

After standing to the southward twenty-four hours the weather moderated, and a warm sun gave us all new life. In another fortnight we passed Sandy

Hook, that seemed to welcome me back to my home. It was the last object I had seen on leaving it, and it was the first to greet me on my return. How unchanged did the long sandy point look with its few scrubby trees and its faithful beacon—but how changed was I !

———

WELL. I had not made a profitless trip to Europe, although it had ended very differently from what I had anticipated when I set out. I had learned how to rough it with the world, and with the elements,—a lesson that I sadly needed. I had preserved my independence and my integrity, and I had improved my health. I had missed seeing the picture galleries of Italy, but I had found something vastly better. I fear that few who go to Europe for improvement, return home with so valuable a stock of experience.

Spite of the hardships I had endured on board the ———, I left her with a feeling of regret; and I could scarce part with my forecastle companions without a tear for the loss of their fellowship. Suffering has a more potent influence in binding men to each other than pleasure.

But the feeling of regret at parting with my shipmates was but slight, compared with my ardent desires to see my friends; and I jumped ashore as soon as the ship struck the dock, proud of my hard hands and weather-beaten appearance, because I could return to my mother without the incumbrance of debt, and better prepared to bear the burden which my loss had imposed upon me, than I was when I left her.

My little narrative is at an end. It is too common-place, I am aware, to deserve notice for its events, since it relates nothing which has not been related before ; but the moral of it is worth having, if the reader can pick it out—if he cannot, it would be idle to do it for him.

Bear in mind, young traveller, when you pine after luxuries that do not happen to be within your reach, that it is possible to endure hard labour and be happy with no other refreshments than potatoes and salt, provided they are honestly earned.

# MUSIC FOR THE MILLION.

## HOMANS & ELLIS,
### NO. 295 BROADWAY, NEW YORK.

HAVE IN PREPARATION THE

# MUSICAL WORLD,
### A SEMI-MONTHLY MAGAZINE

OF

**POPULAR MUSIC FOR THE PIANO FORTE,**
*With occasional Accompaniments for the Flute:*
ach number to contain sixteen pages of elegantly printed Music, for
TWENTY-FIVE CENTS
This series is intended to foster the growing taste for Musical
Knowledge, by the publication of Standard and Classical
Music, at the lowest price consistent with Editorial
accuracy and elegant Typography.

# PIANO-FORTE AND MUSIC STORE

## 295 BROADWAY.

## HOMANS AND ELLIS, (*late Hewitt's*,)

Are sole agents for the sale of Lemuel Gilbert's Patent Action Piano Fortes, manufactured at Boston. They invite the attention of purchasers to the large stock now on hand at 295 Broadway, comprising Rosewood and Mahogany cases, elegantly finished, with six or seven octaves, and possessing all the requisites of the best instruments now made.

Mr. Gilbert has invented an improvement in the action of the Piano Forte, (on which he has secured a patent,) by which great power and beauty of tone, as well as quickness, elasticity, and delicacy of touch, are obtained; at the same time it prevents the liability to get out of order, and thus overcomes the objection to the action of those now in general use. By this invention, performers will find the labor of execution reduced nearly one-half.

*The following letter from Mr. Henry Russell, the Vocalist, expresses an opinion that is entertained by a large number of the Professors of Music in Boston and New-York, and other cities:*

I cannot allow this opportunity to pass, without expressing to you how much delighted I was with Mr. Lemuel Gilbert's Patent Action Pianos. Believe me when I tell you, I was not more delighted than surprised—delighted at the exquisite finish of his Pianos, and surprised at the sweetness of tone they possess. The public should know *this* fact—that for sweetness of tone, for delicacy of expression and touch, for durability of workmanship, for standing long in tune, and for every characteristic which comprises a fine-finished instrument, (strong as the expression may be,) I say it with all sincerity, that for the qualities I have above mentioned, *Mr. Lemuel Gilbert's Pianos stand unrivalled;* and I feel assured in making this acknowledgment, that I am only echoing the sentiments of every *unbiased* professional man in the country.

HENRY RUSSELL.

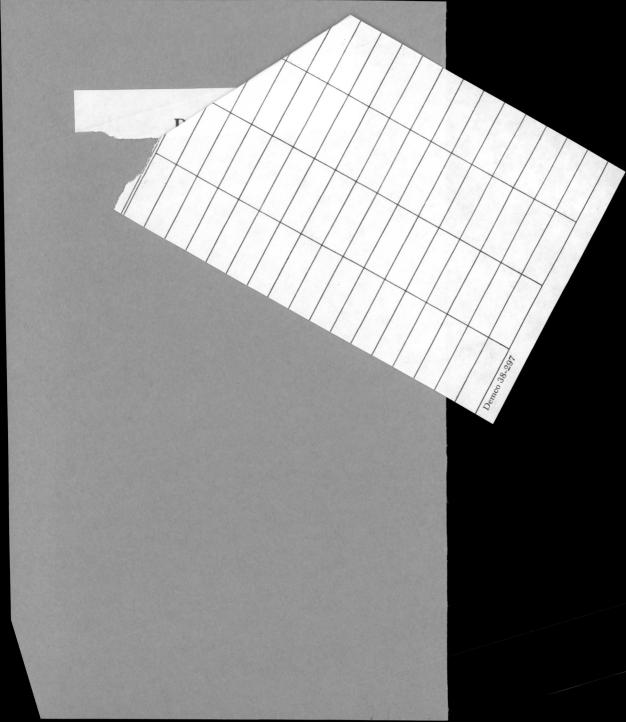